DANGER'S CURE

A HOLLY DANGER NOVEL:
BOOK FOUR

AMANDA CARLSON

DANGER'S CURE

A HOLLY DANGER NOVEL: BOOK FOUR

Copyright © 2017 Amanda Carlson, Inc.

ISBN: 978-1-944431-20-4

OTHER BOOKS BY AMANDA CARLSON

Jessica McClain Series:
Urban Fantasy
BLOODED
FULL BLOODED
HOT BLOODED
COLD BLOODED
RED BLOODED
PURE BLOODED
BLUE BLOODED

Sin City Collectors:
Paranormal Romance
ACES WILD
ANTE UP
ALL IN

Phoebe Meadows:
Contemporary Fantasy
STRUCK
FREED
EXILED

Holly Danger:
Futuristic Dystopian
DANGER'S HALO
DANGER'S VICE
DANGER'S RACE
DANGER'S CURE
DANGER'S HUNT

For Jane.

Chapter 1

"Dammit!" I felt like kicking the side of the medi-pod in frustration, but that would achieve nothing. Instead, I turned in a full circle, hands on my hips.

This one was in worse condition than the last. Not only had the government canceled the project that Roman, the scientist from down South, had been working on to potentially repair the DNA in seekers' bodies from the effects of Plush, but it had annihilated it.

The machines were in pieces.

"We only have two locations left to check," Darby announced as Lockland pried the cover off the front so he could begin to inspect the internal mechanics. After a moment, Darby continued, "There's not a lot we can salvage here." His face was directed inside the pod. "But there are some pieces intact." His hands worked overtime, tugging out parts and dropping them into the box Bender held next to him.

"Do you think you'll have enough?" I asked.

"Enough what? To make a whole machine from scratch?" he asked, his voice muffled. "No. And the key parts—the ones responsible for the actual precision magnetic-field-modulation-based DNA reconstruction—have been completely destroyed. Whoever was doing the damage knew what to do."

Of course they did.

Lockland took a seat on a pile of debris nearby, bowing his head. We were all tired. We'd been at this for the last few days, working around the clock to find these machines, while also trying to dodge strange unmanned aerial crafts, or UACs, that kept popping up all over. It'd been a stamina sucker for everyone involved.

"The last two locations are going to be the riskiest," Lockland said.

I began to pace the small room that used to be a lab of some kind. "Yes, they will be. We decided as a team to try the less-fraught-with-danger locations first, so this is not a surprise." I gestured to the broken medi-pod, which had several large dents pocked in the top, cracked glass, and a control board that had been smashed beyond recognition. "They didn't set any traps for us to find, because they were so confident in the complete destruction of this thing." This particular pod was located outside city limits in an old building we thought the government had used for some kind of experimentation long ago. It was hard to know for sure.

It'd been relatively easy to find, since we had a 3-D map and an eye-diffractor-turned-tracker that blinked when we were within a thirty-meter range.

The last four medi-pods had been found in similar places—broken-down buildings with no locks or obstacles, sitting in a room like this one, thoroughly destroyed and left to rot.

Case walked over, glancing inside the medi-pod. "The most likely location we're going to find a working machine is in the basement of the government building—the one controlled by the Bureau of Truth."

Our investigation into the Bureau of Truth, the secret government agency that'd canceled this much-needed medi-pod program and subsequently ruined these machines, had turned up nothing so far. But it'd been only a few days. I had confidence, especially with Claire on the inside, that we'd get a hold of some information soon.

Waiting wasn't my specialty.

In the notes Roman left behind when he died, he'd said that at least five of the pods had worked. They had completely reversed the damaged DNA of Plush addicts. On the first map we'd discovered, Roman had highlighted a medi-pod in the basement and then labeled the building as headquarters of the Bureau of Truth. Finding an intact medi-pod was the only chance that Mary, and all the other seekers, had to be cured.

"The Bureau of Truth," Bender grumbled. "Whoever the fuck they are. They also have to be the ones tagging us over the last few days. Those drones are hard to shake, too—persistent SOBs." Unfamiliar UACs had popped up outside of Bender's shop and Lockland's residence. They appeared to be military-grade drones—small, sleek, and hard to detect.

"Case is right," I said. "If any medi-pods have been left operational—and you'd think they'd be smart enough to leave at least one working—it would be the one in the building they protect." I moved restlessly around the small space, still contemplating kicking the side of the medi-pod. Purging anger had its benefits, but I refrained.

"Breaching their stronghold is going to be tricky," Lockland said.

Bender growled his agreement.

"But we have no other choice if we want to help Mary and any others," Lockland added.

Mary had become our rallying point. She'd been an innocent caught up in all this, altered by the drug for only a short time, so her prospects for making a full recovery were high, but they were lessening with each passing day.

Darby brought his head out of the machine. "Don't forget that Roman added a note to the 3-D map indicating that that pod was set to be destroyed on 05.07.2159, and it could very well have been." Roman, from what we were able to piece together from the other scientists, had been poisoned, likely by the Bureau of Truth, and ended up dying ten years later from complications from that poison. Before he died, he'd created a tracking program and installed it inside the Eye Diffs, which was how we'd found our way to this place.

If it hadn't been for Roman, we wouldn't be standing here. And without Maisie, our LiveBot status reader, we never would've found the software inside the Eye Diffs. And without the pico, we never would've been able to read them. We had a lot of tech on our side, which was an unusual place for us to be. Most operational tech had been scavenged years ago. I wasn't complaining.

"True, the medi-pod was set to be decimated," I said. "But that doesn't mean they actually did it. Destroying every last one would be a mistake. Years of engineering and brilliant technology went into making those things. Why kill all of them? What if one of their own got infected with Plush? It defies logic not to keep one working."

"I'm not saying I don't agree with you," Darby said. "Those machines would be extremely powerful for healing other ailments, as well. But commandeering that medi-pod will be considered an open act of aggression against our government. And you know as well as I do that if we're caught, we don't live to see another day."

At this point, even though we hadn't officially voted on it as a group, the fact we were all standing here meant we were willing to risk our lives for this cause. Because, quite simply, without actively trying to make the world a better, more sustainable place, we would all die anyway.

It would just take longer, and be quite a bit more miserable.

"You're right." I grinned. "That's why we're not going to get caught."

Darby gave me a wry look as he straightened, shutting the cover panel. "That's it," he said. "I've got everything I can salvage out of this one."

"Look what I found." Daze rushed into the room, his excitement at the forefront. He'd been out investigating the rest of the building, learning how to salvage, and I had to say the kid had a knack for it.

He held his prize aloft.

I walked over to inspect it. He dropped it into my palm, and I brought it closer. "This is a raffie motor." I turned it over. "With all the gears in place. A rare find." I handed it back to him. "Great job. They power household appliances, including some personal-size 3-D bio-printers."

He puffed out his chest in his completely Daze-like way. "It was under a bunch of junk. It took me a while to dig it out. Maisie said there was something else in there, but I couldn't find it."

My eyebrows went up.

Maisie was the status reader Lockland had given us before we'd left on our journey south. She was small and egg-shaped, made of hard polymer. She contained LiveBot technology incorporated with a huge memory file and was learning and adapting to our needs and habits on a daily basis.

The kid kept her close at all times.

If Maisie had made mention of something, it was likely important. "Show us where," I instructed.

Daze led us down a hallway, which was on the way out. Our crafts were parked out front. After two turns, we entered a room with shelving running along one end, possibly used for storage long ago, but it was hard to get a real sense, since everything had disintegrated so badly in our rainy, rusty climate.

Daze held the egg up in the middle of the space like an offering as he intoned in a slightly exaggerated voice, "Detect all like signatures and vital elements, excluding human matter." He was getting good at ordering her around.

We'd realized, after Darby had gotten her to respond to his questions fairly quickly and accurately, that she needed precise directions, or she just kept repeating the same thing over and over again. Detecting like signatures was one of her favorite things to do.

Maisie's kaleidoscope of lights shot around the room, dotting the area with reds, blues, greens, and purples. She used NeuDAR and lidar, which relied on neutrinos and lasers, respectively, to detect both hidden and visible objects. Hence, her light show.

After a moment, her calm robotic voice filled the space. "I detect a high concentration of elemental hydrogen."

Hydrogen usually meant bomb, but not always.

"Are you referring to any of our weapons?" I asked. Most of us used nano-carbon fuel cubes made of compressed hydrogen to power our guns.

Her lights blinked around, her computer brain in action. "Negative. Hydrogen in liquid form."

Bender whistled low, setting the box of parts Darby had collected on the ground. "Liquid fuel. That's not easy to come by or to keep."

He was right. In order to condense hydrogen, it had to be cooled to negative two hundred and forty degrees Celsius at about thirteen atmospheres of pressure and then kept cool in a perfect vacuum. I didn't own a big enough power source to do it myself, although the government did and made limited quantities, as some things still ran on liquid fuel and couldn't be adapted.

Perfect vacuums had been invented about a hundred years ago. They had revolutionized the way people utilized fuel. Hydrogen, and mixed hydrogen bipropellant, had become the norm. But perfect vacuums were almost nonexistent these days, because any minor crack or flaw in the canister caused the compound to decompose immediately.

We needed more information from Maisie. "What's the directional location of liquid hydrogen, Maisie?" I asked the egg.

"Liquid hydrogen detected ten meters south," Maisie replied.

Daze stood in the middle of the room.

We all glanced around, trying to figure out which way was south. We'd been in the building awhile, walking through a bunch of hallways. Not to mention it was always dark outside. Trying to pinpoint directional accuracy when you weren't in your craft with a readout was difficult.

Lockland finally withdrew something from his coat. Then he moved forward, reaching out to touch the wall. He glanced over his shoulder. "This is it. Seven meters south." There was no opening. The wall was solid. "Whatever she's talking about is behind here."

My brow knitted as I moved to stand next to Lockland. "There must've been a room behind here at one time." I examined the wall, knocking to see if there were any particular reverberations. It sounded normal. "If there was, it's been thoroughly sealed." My salvaging instincts took over. "We've got to find a way in. If there's liquid fuel, and it held a vacuum, there might be some other important resources with it." On a few occasions over the years, I'd found rooms that no one else had discovered. But it was exceedingly rare. This had been a government building once upon a time, so who knew what was stored in there? This building would've also been a magnet for early scavengers.

"The entrance could be located on the other side," Bender said as he walked out of the room. "I'll go check."

Darby wandered over to a heap of broken ceiling tiles. "This place is eerie. I wonder what they did here." He picked up a chunk of something and turned it over.

Before any of us could comment, Maisie said, "This location was a treatment facility. Traceable data goes back seventy-five years."

"Treatment of what?" Daze asked what we were all thinking.

"Brain dysfunctions," she answered.

Brain dysfunctions was what our ancestors had called diseases of the mind. No matter how many inoculations the government could engineer, or how many viruses and diseases could be cured with nanobiology, some mental diseases, known from the historical data as "chronic brain dysfunctions," had never been completely resolved.

The conclusion was that people were hardwired when they were born, and no amount of gene therapy could undo biology. "Please don't tell us this facility was used to test human subjects to try and cure brain dysfunctions," I muttered.

"Request to deny information accepted," Maisie said.

Maisie was getting a little creative with her answers. I liked it.

Bender strode in, a macro-sledge over one shoulder, a bare bicep bulging. "There's no other way in, so I stopped at my craft." He made his way to the wall where Lockland stood. "Whatever's behind here, we're about to find out." He lifted the sledge over his head and bashed it directly into the façade.

Chapter 2

It took Bender no more than three swings to create a hole big enough to see through. We all gathered around. The room was black, no light coming from anywhere, making it obvious there had been no other way to enter.

Reaching into my vest pocket, I grabbed my ultra-light and flipped it on, tossing it inside. The interior lit up, exposing the reason why it'd been locked away forever.

Breath escaped Darby's lungs beside me as he stammered, "Are those…are those skeletons?"

Indeed, they were.

Dead bodies had been stacked along all the walls, seemingly in a hurry, and were now just piles of jumbled bones. "Whoever was tasked with sealing up this place didn't care about the dead souls left behind," I said, disgusted. "There's no lingering scent of decay or any stench whatsoever. It just smells musty, like everything else around here. This had to have been done a long time ago."

"Look." Daze stuck his arm through the hole, gesturing toward the wall on the left. "I think that's a medi-pod."

I'd been so focused on the discarded bones, I'd failed to notice the end of a medi-pod sticking out of the wall. This one was horizontal, like the one at the barracks, meant to roll out of the wall. The end carried the telltale symbol of medical aid, a red cross.

"Looks like it," I said.

We all stepped back so Bender could complete the task of decimating the wall, which took only a few more swings. He and Case pried the remaining stubborn pieces away and tossed them behind us.

To enter, we had to step over bones.

The room was bigger than it had seemed looking through the opening, covering about twenty square meters. Bender and Lockland headed toward the medi-pod, while I wandered along the opposite wall, bending down to inspect some of the remains that'd been left so carelessly behind. My stomach churned. These poor souls likely had had no idea what was in store for them when they arrived. There was no way to know if they'd come to this place of their own free will or had been coerced.

In the end, it didn't matter. They were dead and gone.

"How many do you think?" Case asked, stopping beside me.

"My guess is around forty or fifty," I answered. "The government must've panicked. They could've brought these bodies in from other places in the building. Sealing up this room proved to be an efficient way to get rid of all of the evidence in one shot. Who knows? Maybe whatever program they were running was about to be discovered. It's unlikely we'll ever know for sure."

A loud noise clattered behind us as Lockland and Bender tugged the medi-pod free from the wall. I walked over as they rolled it out. Once it was stabilized, we all looked inside. Darby covered his mouth, barely holding back retching noises. Couldn't blame him.

"That's a body," he managed before closing his eyes.

Fully decomposed human remains lay inside. "They were in such a hurry, they didn't even bother to empty the medi-pod before they boarded this place up." I made a gurgling sound in the back of my throat, half disgust, half anger. For the first time, I noticed that the pod had rolled cleanly into the center of the room, which was odd. "How come this thing is so far from the wall? Where's the tether?" I moved to the front of the machine. Most medi-pods had at least one cable attached to the wall or ceiling, where all the wires and electrical connections were housed.

"It looks like this unit is self-powered," Darby said, bending to examine the bottom.

"Self-powered? I didn't think they came like that," I replied.

Lockland knelt next to a side panel and yanked off the metal cover. "Well, now we know what the liquid hydrogen is used for."

I squatted next to him. Sure enough, there were several perfectly intact vacuum canisters tucked inside. "Apparently, standard grid power wasn't enough to get the job done," I said. "But using liquid fuel to power this thing is pretty intense."

"Whatever they were trying to do, they needed a vast amount of output." Darby's voice ended on a stricken note, causing me to glance his way. I watched as he slowly stood, splaying his hands over the top of the clear lid, his eyes glazing over.

In many ways, Darby was the most innocent among us, including Daze. He'd been raised by both his parents, who'd cared deeply for him, until the age of nineteen. He'd been sheltered and lucky enough to have had working tech to foster a fairly robust education.

I rested a hand on his forearm. "What do you think they were doing to these people?" I examined the bones lying around us. "Liquid fuel generates a hell of a lot of power. You don't think this medi-pod was used to fix seekers, do you? And Roman just left it off his list?" It was possible this medi-pod might've been moved. The government was slippery, as evidenced by this walled-up room.

"No, not seekers," Darby replied. "Look." He tapped a finger on the glass lid, his tone miserable.

I glanced down, confused. "What am I supposed to

be seeing?" Some of the bones had fallen to the side during the decaying process.

Case cleared his throat next to me. "I think he's referring to the bones in the middle."

Stark realization hit a moment before my mind fully computed the scene before me. I gasped, horrified. "She was pregnant?" The pile of bones in the middle of the skeleton were so tiny, they were almost barely there. There was a small skull no bigger than my fist resting on the pelvic bone. "Do you think they were trying to alter a fetus in utero?" Along with the quest for perfect health, our ancestors had been obsessed with unmarred appearances. The evidence was everywhere—in the setup of their homes, in the amount of money spent on augmentations and beauty products. Unborn genetic selection had been fairly common. A program called YOUborn, where the parents could select everything from hair and eye color, to skin tone, to size and build, was available, but it'd basically been restricted to the elite because the cost was so high.

If you didn't fit into the world's definition of perfect, your existence must've been difficult.

"That's fucked up," Bender said.

I took a step back, and a long, tired breath trailed out. "They created an extremely powerful medi-pod, powered by rocket fuel, to try and alter fetuses? For what purpose? Did these women know what they were doing?" My eyes rested on the other skeletons littered around the room, dumped without care, picking out tons of tiny bones, something my brain hadn't computed before. They'd all been pregnant. "Didn't anyone miss them?"

"That's something we can never know," Darby said. "And yes, these women likely thought they were doing what was best for their unborn children. At the time, there were comprehensive DNA tests that could be done noninvasively on a fetus as young as several weeks old. Some of the kits could even be purchased at a local merchant and completed at home. My guess is these women found out their child was carrying a certain mutation, and they sought help to try to fix it."

"Could be," I said, glancing around, "but there are so many. It doesn't make sense that the government could amass this many pregnant women, kill them, and just wall them up never to be found again without someone discovering the crime. They should've been missed by their families—by *someone*. Meaning there should've been a record of this. It should've been a scandal. Fifty pregnant women gone missing is newsworthy."

"Not if the government was extremely selective in their process," Case muttered next to me, his voice echoing the disgust that still roiled through me.

"Selective how?" I asked.

"Making sure these women were loners who no one would miss," he answered. "If the government really wanted to cover their tracks and make sure this was never discovered, they would've incinerated the bones. That's how all bodies were dealt with after death. Instead, they figured this would be enough."

My stomach clenched. "If they were loners…they

probably weren't pregnant when they arrived." Surely their partners would've had something to say about their unborn babies going missing. "That means these women were likely lured here and purposely impregnated with embryos that had known DNA mutations. So the government could experiment on fixing the problem?"

Darby coughed, taking a step away from the medi-pod. "That could very well be what happened. The government, as well as private companies, was constantly trying to bribe people to be part of human scientific studies, which were happening all the time. It was against the law to do any testing without consent, but if you had permission, you could do anything. There was a high court decision that established this as law more than one hundred years ago. It concluded that humans, at the age of adulthood, could make informed decisions themselves without interference from the government."

"Ignoring the fact that most people would do just about anything to stay alive," I huffed. "Including signing their bodies away for enough coin to put a roof over their heads. Living in a megascraper was expensive, and everything people needed was tied up in technology, which didn't run cheap. There were definitely people living on the outskirts." Just like there were now. On the shell, our ancestors' world might have projected beauty, efficiency, and progress, but on the inside, it'd been almost devoid of empathy and feeling for those who couldn't compete.

"Nobody cared about people without means," Lockland said. "That was clear enough in the history left behind. The government provided housing for the poorest and gave people basic necessities, but from what I've read, those neighborhoods were like war zones. People preferred to be homeless, rather than live in fear."

"Prior to the meteor strikes," I said, "people were exiting the city in droves. The Rural Plan started ten years before Earth was shattered. According to what was left behind, rural areas consisted of 3-D-printed homes that were affordable. If you had a bio-printer, access to slurry, and a roof over your head, you were better off than in the city."

"That did happen," Darby concurred. "And the government considered the Rural Plan to be a success. But there was hardly any work outside the city, so there was almost no opportunity to earn a wage. Existence must've been very utilitarian. Every single thing our ancestors manufactured, they did with automation and robots."

I ran a hand over the top of the medi-pod. "Well, we can hypothesize all day about what happened here, but we're never going to know the truth. These poor souls are dead and gone, and there's nothing we can do and nobody left who cares." It was a shame all around. I addressed Darby. "Now that you've gathered more parts, is there any way to insert them into this medi-pod? It runs on rocket fuel. It would certainly have enough power to handle a DNA conversion."

Darby shrugged. "Of course, having a working pod makes things easier than building one from scratch. But the key will be finding an intact control panel, if possible. That's what holds all the software—what the engineers and scientists were working on for all those years. A program that would direct a magnetic field to read and rework the damaged DNA. Without that, the technology might be lost forever."

I nodded. "I think the chance of finding one is high. It would've been incredibly stupid to destroy them all. All that engineering for nothing. It was the kind of work that could not possibly be replicated in our lifetimes." To destroy those capabilities forever seemed unthinkable. I turned to Lockland. "There's no way we're giving this machine up, so we need to figure out a way to transport it to the Emporium. If we leave it here, we run the risk of someone else discovering it." We weren't the only salvagers in the city. But the medi-pod was too huge to be hauled by any of our crafts.

Lockland gave me a look, a cross between pain and acceptance. "The mover drone in Port Station is the only craft I know of that could get the job done." Pain, because the mover drone was going to be hard to retrieve. Acceptance, because we'd do it anyway.

"I figured as much," I said. "Just making sure you didn't have something categorically simpler as a better option."

Bender stood with one arm on the pod. "We're going to need that mover drone for a whole slew of things in the immediate future. I say we go in and take it. The sooner the better."

Lockland ran a hand around the back of his neck. "Once we do, we break all ties with Port Station for good and become their enemy. It will cut off our current informant relationships, too. We're setting ourselves up for a constant ongoing battle with them, so we do it carefully."

"There might be a better way to handle it," Case said.

Surprised, we all glanced at the outskirt. "They're not giving that drone up willingly," I said. "It's too valuable. I'm on Bender's side. We go in and take it. In my mind, they have it coming. After all, they took Luce hostage without worrying about pissing us off." Case and I had liberated my craft from Port Station a short time ago, which had involved weapons and deadly force. "I also haven't forgotten they put an explosive tracker on her."

"Yeah," Bender said. "That thing was a bitch to get off."

"I agree," Case said. "We take it. But before we do, we can at least try to negotiate with them. It would make our lives easier, and I think we have something they might be willing to take in trade, at least for a while."

"Yeah, and what's that?" I asked, knowing he wasn't talking about coin.

Case inclined his head at me. "Your E-unit should suffice."

Chapter 3

Everyone started talking at once. I held up my hand, my eyes rolling toward the ceiling.

"What E-unit?" Bender demanded.

"You have an E-unit?" Lockland asked.

"You told him about your E-unit?" Darby said.

"What's an E-unit?" Daze asked.

My lofted arm did nothing to stop the barrage of chatter.

Maisie's voice cut through the melee with her calm, soothing cadence. "An E-unit, otherwise known as an electrolysis unit, separates hydrogen and oxygen atoms from water using a strong electrical current. The objective is to harness hydrogen gas, compressing it for later use. Pure oxygen is an asset in our world and can be used for a variety of things."

"Yes, we know what an E-unit is," Bender grumbled. "We just didn't know Holly has one."

My eyes rested firmly on Case. "Look, I know you

haven't been around for very long, so you're entitled to a modicum of leeway, but you should've known better." He really should have. Even though he hadn't been formally voted into our group, he'd earned his spot through his actions. But the man was still on probation. "In this group, we keep things private—for a reason. Now that everyone knows I have an E-unit, it puts them in danger. There's a government here, unlike where you came from, and the more we know about each other, the more we risk. It shouldn't have to be spelled out to you." Without waiting for him to respond, I turned to Lockland and Bender. "Yes, I have an E-unit. And yes, I showed it to Darby recently. When it's at optimal capacity, I can produce five hundred kilojoules of energy in the form of compressed hydrogen per day. I store much of what I produce in cubes, but I have multiple pressure vessels as well. I was forced to show the E-unit to Case that day we met Tandor at the gorge, after you two had been kidnapped. I needed to pick up a stash of hydro-bombs and was forced to bring the outskirt with me."

Lockland crossed his arms. "A working E-unit at that capacity is impressive. I think Case might be right. Something like that coupled with a box of empty carbon bombshells, which I have, to avoid war with Port Station might be a better option. I could negotiate a month of time with the mover drone in exchange for their ability to make weapons."

"I'm not sure I agree," I hedged. "Lending them an E-unit and shells to make bombs would mean arming

Port Station. If things in our world change, and we find ourselves going up against them in the future, their firepower would be increased a hundredfold, thanks to us. That seems counterintuitive to me."

"I don't know," Darby said from his position next to me. "If we offer them something of value, we align ourselves with them before the de facto government has a chance to do the same. If the Bureau of Truth realizes they're outnumbered, they would probably look to Port Station for help. If we get their allegiance first, it could benefit us."

I nodded. "I see your point, and that might be a good idea *if* they agree. But as of late, we haven't exactly been on good terms with them." Tandor's group had infiltrated their ranks, and we were unsure what the environment in Port Station was now.

Bender ducked through the hole in the wall, and the rest of us followed. "I like it," he said. "I have a bad feeling about this government group. With the UACs popping up all over, it proves they've been watching us for a while. A battle is brewing. If we set ourselves up with Port Station, it can better situate us for a win."

Lockland said, "That settles it. I'll set up a meet with my connection and offer him the deal. We'll go from there."

"Okay," I said, not pointing out that I hadn't yet agreed to go along with forfeiting my E-unit, even temporarily. It'd been Case's idea, not mine. The thought of something happening to it was a little out of my comfort zone, but I was willing to go along with it for the greater good. "When you meet, make sure you set conditions with them. If anything happens to my unit, we get something of greater value in return. We're not risking it for nothing."

Lockland moved toward the door of the room we were in. "Will do. I'm heading out first. If I encounter any UACs, I'll send out an alert. Keep your phones close for an update." Then he disappeared through the opening.

Darby, Daze, and I had arrived in Luce. Bender, Case, and Lockland had each taken their own crafts. Bender had begun pulling things in front of the hole to prevent anyone else from discovering the medi-pod. Case joined in.

"Can you handle this by yourselves?" I asked.

"What do you think?" Bender grunted.

"Just trying to be polite," I said. "I'm taking Darby and Daze back to the Emporium to check on Mary, and then I'm heading to my place in the canals to get some sleep." It'd been a long day. By the time we arrived back in the city, it would be the beginning of blackout. "We rendezvous in the morning at the Emporium." It'd become our new headquarters of sorts, especially since Bender's place was being monitored by UACs.

Case grabbed some broken shelving units, sliding them in front of the other stuff. The hole was almost covered. "We're almost done here."

"I'll take this with us." I hefted up the box full of salvageable parts Darby had pulled from the medi-pod, then the three of us headed out the door and down the hallway.

Once outside, Darby and Daze headed to the passenger side of Luce and got in. I opened the pilot side and handed the box into the backseat to Daze. "I'm halfway through Roman's notes," Darby told me as he strapped himself in. "I'm hoping to find something more valuable than historical data and locations, but so far that's all there is."

"I'm sure the kid can help you," I said, starting Luce up, my toe in the failsafe position under the front of the dash. Her props sputtered to life. "How about you spend the night with Darby?" I glanced over my shoulder at Daze. "Then you can both go over those notes together. You can sleep on one of the pallets there." Having some alone time suddenly sounded extremely nice. Up until becoming Daze's sustainer, I'd spent most of my time alone. Lately, not so much. It would be nice to have a break.

Daze nodded eagerly. "I like Darby's lab. It's fun there."

"Perfect," I said.

Maisie's voice came out of Daze's pocket as I lofted Luce into the air. "I detect no humans or unidentifiable crafts in the area." Maisie had learned that upon takeoff, we always asked her for stats. Now she provided them on her own, which was helpful.

"Thanks, Maisie," I said. "I appreciate the update."

"I enjoy being helpful," she replied. "Rain is falling. It is fifteen degrees Celsius. It's advisable to bring an umbrella. Helmets may be insufficient."

Darby chuckled. "I think she's developing a sense of humor. Whoever wrote this program was brilliant. Her adaptations and quirks are becoming more personalized each day."

"I'm not sure I can handle an inanimate polymer egg cracking jokes all the time," I said as I checked the gauges on the dash. I trusted Maisie, but growing dependent on an object that could break, shatter, or cease to exist at any time wasn't advisable. "Do you think all status readers share the same software?"

"I'm not really sure," Darby answered. "But I wouldn't assume so. There had to be hierarchies. In the marketplace, they probably priced them according to how specialized and intricate their systems were. If this is a military-grade status reader, it probably has the very best software available at the time. Honestly, Lockland was incredibly lucky to find it. I still can't believe we have one."

Daze positioned himself between the two front seats, his face jutting through. "I don't think it was luck."

"Why not?" I asked, scanning the sky. My tech phone hadn't made any noise, which was good. We'd all agreed to reenter the city from different directions. I didn't usually come in over the water south of the canals, but I was going to attempt it today. Flying with Case had gotten me used to being over the sea. This wasn't open ocean. I could handle it.

"I mean, it was lucky he found it," Daze clarified. "A salvage like that is always amazing." He was certainly right about that. "But I'm pretty sure military-grade status readers were the only ones that could've survived this long. Regular status eggs were made with a more brittle polymer and had no protective coating. At least, that's what it said on my dad's pico."

"I bet someone would know that for sure," I said. "Have you asked Maisie?"

The kid's face fell as his expression turned to wonder. "I didn't think of that."

I chuckled. "Don't worry. I'm right there with you. It's going to take us some time to get used to having a full data bank of information whenever we need it." Daze slid into the backseat, murmuring to Maisie. I turned to Darby. "How is Mary doing?"

I'd checked on her every day since we'd returned. Ned was a constant, thank goodness, hovering over her, feeding her, and making sure she didn't hurt herself. Keeping her ankles and wrists secured sucked, but it was still necessary.

"Her situation is worsening. I know you're against it, but I really think we should give her some Plush." Darby had recovered a few doses from the lab where he'd worked for Tandor. They hadn't manufactured it there, but they'd used it as a baseline when he'd thought he was involved in finding a chemical cure. I wasn't interested in giving Mary more of the drug, and we'd gotten into a few arguments over it already.

He held up his hand. "I know what you're going to say, but hear me out. Her DNA is already damaged. Giving her the drug would calm her down and let her body finally get some rest. Continuing to live in this heightened state is going to harm her. She doesn't sleep much, and Ned has a hard time feeding her. It seems like it's the most humane thing we can do, and it might give her a greater chance of survival in the long run. Her body is wearing out, Hol. We have to do something."

"I understand," I said. "You've explained it all before. But we're so close to finding a working medi-pod." At least, I hoped we were. "Giving her more Plush now risks altering her DNA even more."

Darby nodded. "It might, but not having it is doing equal—if not greater—damage. There's a reason why the government continued to provide addicts with Plush. It kept the seekers as sane as they could be. She's just short of losing her mind completely, which a medi-pod won't be able to put back together."

I sighed. "Okay, okay. But give her a small dose and monitor her throughout the night."

"I will," he said. "It's the right thing to do. Even though I know it's a hard choice."

I banked Luce to the east, beginning the first turn that would take us over the water, hitting the canals from the south. Still no sign of anything in the air. "I don't trust these new UACs," I muttered. "They're sneaky. Even if they're not in the sky, they could be parked on top of a building, recording us."

Three separate beeps sounded at once.

All of our tech phones were going off.

Shit.

Darby withdrew his. Lockland's voice came through the speaker. "It's Larry. I'm running an errand," he said. "Picking up something from nine. See you in the morning at Mary's house."

"Dammit," I muttered. That meant he'd picked up a UAC, likely outside his residence. He was telling us he was heading to safe house number nine for the night. "Mary's house" was the Emporium.

Before Darby could respond, Lockland continued, "I'll bring you something back. Talk later." The phone went dark, meaning he'd shut off the connection on his end so we wouldn't reply.

"What did he mean by 'bring you something back'?" Daze asked, scooting between the seats again.

"He was telling us that he can handle this on his own," I said. "'I'll bring something back' means you got it covered. If you need backup, you tell *us* to bring something—like, 'Meet me at nine and bring a protein cake.' And if it's a huge emergency and you need immediate assistance, you tell us something has already been delivered—like, 'I'm at nine, and there's a box on the doorstep.'"

"Cool," Daze said. "I think somebody would have a hard time understanding what you meant if they didn't know the code."

"That's the point, kid." I chuckled as we began soaring over water. The sea was roiling with two-to-three-meter swells, nothing like the open ocean. Even though it was tamer, I certainly wouldn't want to crash in it.

"The meaning is twisted enough," he said, "but not too much. If anyone was listening, they would think it was much more complicated than it actually is."

"You're right. It's not exactly a code. It's more of a language—one that we don't even specify much anymore because we're so used to it. If Lockland chose different words, but articulated it in the same way, I would understand him. After all our years together, our original code has morphed into something more nuanced. I'm sure you'll pick it up soon."

Daze bobbed his head up and down. "I think I already have. After all, we've spent *a lot* of time together in the last few weeks."

"Yes, we have," I said. *And that's why a sleepover with Darby is such an excellent idea.*

Chapter 4

I exited my cleaning stall feeling halfway decent and, for the first time in a long while, hopeful there might be a possibility of working my way back to my normal self—if normal was possible again. So much had happened in such a short amount of time, my mind constantly churned through everything, weighing all the pros and cons, trying to formulate plans necessary to save my crew and the inhabitants of this city, never getting much of a break. It kept me in a constant state of alertness.

A peaceful night in my sleeping pod would revitalize me further, especially since I was finally clean. I'd almost forgotten what that felt like, but damn, it was nice.

I padded over to an integrated drawer and pulled out a fabric T-shirt that was so worn it was almost see-through in some places, making it exquisitely soft, and a pair of shorts of the same material. The material was so old, I didn't even have a name for what it was. I'd salvaged them both a long time ago.

Slipping them on, I sighed, pulling my semidry hair out of the collar, letting it fall around my shoulders. These had been called pajamas once upon a time. My ancestors had had the luxury of wearing different clothes to sleep in, a different pair each night. The idea was absurd. My mother had loved wearing them. I distinctly remember the look of glee on her face when we would stumble on them during our salvages together. My mother had not been an expert salvager, by any means, never venturing into a space that was compromising, but she'd taught me enough. And sometimes we'd gotten lucky.

Glancing down, I smoothed the fabric, enjoying how it felt under my gloveless hands. It was a rarity to relax, especially in this heightened climate, but there was a high probability I wouldn't see a night like this for months, so I planned to enjoy it.

It was a little cold with my arms and legs exposed, but I'd trade a little temperature discomfort for the softness against my skin. I made my way into the living area, picking a bag of protein flakes off the counter where Daze had stacked them, missing Walt's bio-printed food, my mouth immediately salivating as I thought about his delicious cupcakes.

Tasting them had brought new meaning to the way I viewed what I put in my mouth. It had been revolutionary, and I couldn't wait to get the scientists back here so we could have food like that to eat every day.

Using an ultrasonic whisk, I busied myself heating up water and pouring it into the bag, idly spooning the meal into my mouth as my brain began replaying everything we had to do moving forward. I finished the tasteless protein mush in a few bites and threw the pouch into my grinder, listening to the slow whir of the motor as it tore up the packaging.

Once upon a time, the grinder would've separated things on a molecular level. Everything in this building had been recycled and reused—water, garbage, and waste—flushed down pipes to the bottom level, where huge bins collected the contents and continued the separation process, filtering everything based on weight and chemical composition, sending it to their new destinations to be consumed again, in a seemingly never-ending process. My building was one of the many megascrapers that had dotted the city skyline, providing the texture and flow of this massive, bustling metropolis. Every megascraper built in the last hundred years had been self-sufficient, meant to last into the next century or longer. Too bad they hadn't been built to withstand unforeseen titanic events.

Just as I was turning off the lights, one of my alarms sounded, the red light by my front door beginning to flicker.

Someone was trying to get in.

"Hell." I rushed down the hall, plucking up my Gem from the shelf by the door. The blinking red light meant that whoever was here was on my balcony, where my E-unit was located. I had a bunch of traps set, so the likelihood of anyone getting this far should have been low.

I slapped my palm against the heat sensor. The door popped open and I entered the hallway, my back flat against the wall, my hand wrapped around my weapon, my elbows tucked close to my body.

It took me less than thirty seconds to arrive at the entrance that led to my balcony. I stopped, listening. No sound, and none of my other alarms had been tripped. Nor had there been an explosion, followed by howls of pain.

I waited a full three minutes. Nothing. No noise and no pattering from the roof above me. All was quiet. "If somebody's playing a trick on me, they're willing to pay a pretty high price," I muttered as I moved forward, throwing the inside bolt and easing the door open, standing to the side, ducking my head around the jamb.

All clear.

That meant nobody had tried to open the door to my balcony into this small entryway. If they had, they would've been blown up. That also meant that whoever was out there was likely still there. As I crept forward, I recognized that there was a slight possibility my laser alarm had been trigged by falling debris, but that was doubtful.

It'd never happened before, though there was always a first time.

My balcony was fifty-something stories up, so there were limited ways to get here. Whoever was out there would've had to have used a craft and then rappelled down from the roof, or used the cable swing connected to the building next door, which was hidden fairly well.

The craft was out, because I would've heard the landing above me, so it had to be the cable swing.

Stopping just before the door that would lead me to my prey, I rested my helmetless head against the wall. I wore my ridiculous pajamas—I hadn't had time to change—no helmet, no synthetic leather, just me, my soft T-shirt and shorts, bare feet, and semiwet hair. It felt strange. I didn't have any amplifiers set up on the balcony, so my listening wouldn't be foolproof.

No sound came from inside that I could detect.

I slid my hand just above the lever, placing my palm firmly against the cold metal. Once the heat sensor engaged, a small click sounded. Whoever was on the other side would have heard it if they were listening carefully.

At this point, I could announce myself, or I could just whip open the door, hoping to take them by surprise.

I decided to go with the whip-open-the-door plan.

Once it swung wide, I pivoted in front, extending my arms, my Gem out, a *don't fuck with me* expression firmly planted in place. "Don't move if you plan on living," I announced in a low, gravelly tone meant to convey anger and incite fear. It took me only a second to see who it was. I lowered my weapon. "What the hell are you doing out here, Case? You just came precariously close to dying."

The outskirt was perched on the edge of my balcony, body angled back, posture relaxed, arms crossed, like he had just dropped in for a visit.

He stood. "I didn't have enough battery power in my craft to make it back to the barracks," he said by way of explanation. "So I came here." He shrugged.

I shouldn't be surprised.

Case was nothing but unpredictable. I had a few options, one of which was not letting him in and forcing him to sleep in his craft, which sounded tempting, but I wasn't a monster. Since he was already here, and clearly knew this was my residence, I might as well let him in.

Sighing, I gestured toward two of my traps on the ground near the door. "Step over those and follow what I do exactly." Once we were in the hallway, I shut the door, placing my hand on the sensor to trigger the connection. I moved ahead. "Stay in the middle, don't bump into any walls." He followed without comment. Out in the main hallway, I tossed over my shoulder, "Close that door behind you and turn your back." Even though I was about to bring him into my home, he wasn't going to see how I unlocked my door. "Honestly, Case, what were you thinking?" I muttered, half under my breath, half not. "We have phones for these kinds of things. Why risk landing on my balcony unannounced and blowing yourself up?"

The door opened, and I went inside, not waiting for him to catch up.

He ducked through a moment later, a second before the door would've latched and he would've spent the night in the hallway. "I don't have a handle," he replied as he made his way into my personal space. "The plan was to take my craft to the barracks after stopping at the Emporium, but the battery light went red in the air. This was the closest destination." He glanced around. "Nice place."

I grunted as I set my Gem back on the shelf. "It is." I moved toward my living area and leaned into the doorjamb, crossing my arms, partly to try to conceal the fact that I wore a pair of threadbare pajamas—which was next to impossible to hide, as my legs and arms were completely exposed—and partly because I was irritated. "And I'd like to keep it that way. So, just to make sure we share a similar understanding, you're not going to blow this place up once you leave, right?" The thought had crossed my mind.

"No," Case said. "And I didn't blow up your other residence."

"But you knew they were going to do it." It wasn't a question. I dropped my arms and reached in, turning on the lights, making my way to my cooling unit to grab some water. "Kind of makes you guilty all the same. That's why you were trying to find me in The North, wasn't it?"

"Yes," he answered, following me into the living area.

I poured myself a cup, then turned, bracing my hips against the counter. "How did they time it so perfectly?" I took a sip, not offering him any.

"I sent them a signal," he said with absolutely zero shame in his voice.

"You cut it pretty close. The craft almost got caught up in it." I glanced at him over the rim, conveying my disdain.

He nodded as he took a seat on the bench in front of my wall screen, still managing to make it seem like dropping by my residence was a common occurrence. He appeared tired and weary, just like me. I watched as his gaze found its way to my wall of batteries. His expression remained steady, but I saw his eyes go tight at the corners. He hadn't expected me to have this many resources. The wall *was* pretty impressive. He found my gaze again, tugging his helmet off, running a gloved hand through his hair, making it stick up all over. "They wanted me to kill you. I refused."

"If you're expecting a thank-you, it'll be a very long wait. Like, an eternity of waiting," I grunted. "So long, in fact, you'll perish first. So, instead of killing me, you blew up my house. Makes sense." It made no sense.

"Yes. No." He shook his head, frustrated. *You're not alone, Case.* "If I hadn't done it, they were going to kill you, then Daze."

"Was that before or after I was slated to be their next Plush-addicted sex slave?" I pushed off the counter, grabbing the water jug. "You know…" I walked over to a direct water spigot hollowed out in the wall, twisted the cap of the jug off, and placed it under the faucet and lifted the lever. As water poured in, I continued, "Nothing you've said has ever really added up. You knew Tandor, you were cozy with Hutch, you have access to military locations and supplies. You tell one story, only to contradict it by another. You've managed to secure a place in our crew, having aided me more than three times, but that doesn't mean we trust you. Trust is earned."

"By aided, do you mean saved?"

I spun toward him, irritated, water sloshing to the floor. "Shit." I turned off the spigot by twisting the valve and faced Case. "Do you really want to argue about what saving a life means?" A moment later, I spotted the edge of his mouth slightly turning up. His way of making a joke. "It's nice you like to bait me. Blow up my home, push me out a two-story window, act like you rescued me—"

He stood suddenly, surprising me, almost causing me to drop the full jug. His face stayed angled toward the floor, his legs splayed, his expression tight.

"What?" I asked when he didn't say anything. "What's going on?"

"I'm not trying to bait you." Very slowly, he lifted his head, gray eyes piercing mine. Emotion swirled just beneath the surface, something Case didn't usually allow to penetrate his carefully constructed veneer. "What they did to Frankie was almost too much for me to bear. I wasn't going to let that happen again, so I did what I thought was..." He trailed off, glancing around the room, appearing to have lost his thoughts for a moment.

I had a choice. I could continue to argue with him, trying to get him to admit to his mistakes—which were vast—or I could put him out of his misery. I wasn't usually generous when it came to these things, but seeing that we'd spent so many days together in the last two weeks, I had a pretty good idea that he wasn't out to get me and that his bad decisions weren't always made with ill intent.

Plus, if I gave him some leeway now, I could use it against him later when I made him work to salvage all the things he'd blown up. "Do you want to spray off?" I asked, changing the subject. "Looks like you could use it. The cleaning stall is down the hall to the right." I gestured toward my sleeping room.

His gaze shot to mine. He was startled by the direction the conversation had taken.

I had to admit—but not to him—I was, too.

Chapter 5

Since I'd allowed Case the use of my cleaning stall, which he'd taken advantage of, seemingly happy with the distraction I'd so graciously offered, I'd been relegated to staying in the living area.

All I really wanted to do was go to bed, but the sleeping pods were situated less than three meters from the cleaning stall. That wasn't happening until he was out.

The only thing to do in this compact space was to eat and drink, which I'd already done, or sit back on my integrated seating and watch my wall screen, which was what I was doing. It was easy to get lost in the sky and the wispy clouds floating over the mysterious white building I would never see in person. The scene always calmed me in ways I didn't understand, the vapor of the clouds so thin the crystalline-blue backdrop seeped through. I couldn't believe our sky beyond the clouds was that color. It seemed like a sick joke that such beauty was hovering above us, but we'd never be able to see it.

I was so caught up in the video that I didn't hear the door to the cleaning stall open. The first thing I noticed were footsteps coming toward me. I lifted my head off the crook of my elbow, where it had been lying comfortably.

Case was naked from the waist up.

As he walked, he rubbed his hair with a small cloth to help along the drying process. My stall wasn't great at the drying part. The heater required more power to operate than I had connected, thusly it didn't produce as much hot air as it would've back in the day, when the unit ran at full power.

I sputtered as I sat up, swinging my feet to the cool floor, refusing to flinch as my bare feet came in contact with the ground. "Where are your clothes?" I asked. More like demanded. I'd rarely seen Case without his trench since the first night we met, when I'd broken his nose. That seemed like a lifetime ago. I stood. "I mean…where is your shirt?" I gestured at his bare chest, because it gave me something to do instead of stand there awkwardly. "Because, clearly, you have pants on."

His pants were made of synthetic leather, like mine, and hugged every contour of his massive thighs. His chest rippled with strength, showing off his well-defined muscles, a set of broad shoulders, and a coating of brown curly hair that tapered into four solid, identifiable rows of abs, ending somewhere beneath his waistband.

I'd seen Bender without a shirt many times, and if I had to wager, Case might have him beat in sheer muscle definition, if not mass. There were lots of shadows happening.

He ignored my babbling as he continued to dry his hair, his eyes darting to the screen. "What's that?"

With relief, I tore my eyes off his chest and repositioned them on the screen. It was just a human body, after all. People traditionally *did* take their clothes off when they entered a cleaning stall. The objective was to wash naked body parts, not parts covered by trench coats and other stuff. Case was still wet, hence the cloth in his hand and the leftover droplets on his chest.

"It's a working wall screen." I picked up the remote. "It has four different programmed settings." I flicked through them slowly. Rolling green hills with grazing horses; colorful flowers with bees buzzing—my least favorite because of the noise; a large mountain crag with its clear-sky backdrop, swaying, lush green trees, and pristine snowcap; and the white building with the flittering white clouds. "It popped to life after I installed a sonic-wave monitor. I connected some loose wires, and it worked. Darby thinks it's incredible because this kind of tech has a limited life-span. Something about the pixels drying up over time."

Case came to a stop next to me, our shoulders almost touching. His bare skin radiated heat next to my soft-fabric-clad body. I resisted pulling away, but just barely. The turn of events in the last half hour had been bizarre.

He continued to dry his neck and upper torso. "It is incredible," he murmured. "I've never seen a working unit."

"Yeah," I said distractedly, handing him the remote. "Feel free to utilize it. I'm going to get some rest, which is what I came here for." I moved around him and headed down the hall, careful not to seem like I was fleeing, which, if truth be told, I was. Over my shoulder, I called, "You can sleep on the bench seat. There's a blanket in one of the drawers, or"—I considered not offering this option, but clearly he'd already seen it—"there's another sleeping pod in here." Sweat pooled under my arms as I walked. I was glad Maisie wasn't here to tattle on me, which was one of her favorite things to do. She seemed to enjoy blaring my statistics to anyone who would listen, racing heart rates being a personal fave. Who knew what she would've said now, but I was relieved I didn't have to find out.

As I climbed into my sleeping pod, it perturbed me that I'd allowed Case to have such an effect on me. All he'd done was come out of the cleaning stall with a bare chest, and suddenly air was having a hard time exiting my lungs.

Case entered the room, and I ignored him, busying myself getting organized. I'd picked up my Gem on the way, and I'd already had my taser in here. Most of the time, I slept with the lid up, but tonight I'd planned to close it because I was in desperate need of a dose of UV.

In this world, you died without enough UV. But I couldn't close the lid with Case here. I needed to be able to hear any and all movements.

I'd have to deal with the UV in the morning.

After a few more moments of trying to find a comfortable position, I felt like hauling my ass out and putting on my leathers. I'd probably get more sleep on the seating bench in the living area. It was clear my stolen night of relaxation had been hijacked by the outskirt, and instead of feeling at peace, I felt exposed and uneasy.

My pod door was up, which blocked Case's movements on the other side, but I heard him getting in. After that, everything quieted down. Case had doused the lights when he entered the room, so other than the soft glow of the control panel near my head, there was no light to see by.

If my heart rate slowed anytime soon, I might be able to get some rest.

After several more minutes, it was abundantly clear sleep would be evasive. I decided to break the silence, figuring the outskirt was awake as well. Talking was better than lying in silence. "What was Frankie like?"

"He was younger than Daze, around the same height." Case's voice came out in a soft growl, the kind of sound you made after a contented yawn. "He had dark hair and eyes. He was funny and full of empathy. He was the definition of what was still worth living for in this world."

"Sounds like he had a big impact on you," I said. After all, what happened to the kid had changed the entire course of Case's life. If Case hadn't chosen to seek his revenge on those who killed Frankie, he wouldn't be here right now.

"He did."

"If he hadn't been murdered, do you think you would've stayed with your tribe?" I'd gotten a tiny glimpse of his old hometown when we'd dealt with Freedom, his sustainee brother, who was crazy insane, along with his three wives and a bunch of children living in a shack near the sea.

"I don't know," he replied. "I didn't have a plan. Dixon died four months prior to my return there, so everything was up in the air."

"Tell me about your time with Dixon," I said. "It's clear you guys covered a lot of ground during your travels. You were with him for a while, right?"

"Yes." His voice was tight. "We were together seven years."

When more didn't come, I prodded, "He was your mentor, correct? He spared you alone that night when he took all those other militia men out. He had to have shared some of his past with you. After all, he showed you the barracks and that cave where we found the Eye Diffs." I was surprised that communicating like this, separated by the darkness, was easier than talking to Case face-to-face. If Case was going to confide anything to me and finally open up about his past, it would be now.

"He told me bits and pieces." His tone was modulated. Maybe not.

"Things you aren't willing to share?" I asked.

"Not yet."

"Why?"

No response.

"How do you expect us to trust you—"

"I can't tell you." A hint of desperation echoed there, but I chose to ignore it. "For the same reason you keep your information secure from your crew. Some things are just…too personal."

I snorted. I couldn't help it. "Personal like my E-unit? You're here, in my home, uninvited, telling me you can't confess certain parts of your life after you blabbed my secrets to the group?" With the uptick in my voice and the sudden feeling of vulnerability, my arms sprang apart, striking the sides of the pod, making an echoing noise around the room.

Clutching them back together, I reclasped them across my stomach so they would stay put. Dammit. My heart rate had slowed, but now it was back to pulsing in my ears.

"I didn't mean to expose your secrets," he answered softly, almost too quietly for me to hear. "I figured something like that was known to the group. It's a valuable asset."

"I know what it's worth," I retorted, a little mollified, heart rate slowing. I paused, thinking about how things had played out tonight. "Why didn't you call me on the tech phone and tell me you were here?

The handle excuse was bullshit. We both know it. I would've recognized your voice."

An eternity seemed to pass before he spoke again. "Because you would've told me no."

Breath caught in my chest right in the middle of exhaling, my heart pounding again. I had to focus on taking in a regular breath so I didn't start coughing or sputtering like I was having some sort of seizure. I gripped my hands even tighter to keep them still.

Just hearing Case's voice, not being able to see his expressions, I began to understand his cadence and his word choices like I never had before. When he was evasive or didn't want to answer my questions, his tone was matter-of-fact, sometimes—*many* times— ending on a steely note. When he was genuinely concerned, or responded in a manner I would consider sincere, his voice dropped and his words became infused with something mimicking emotion.

I assumed the outskirt was mimicking, because I wasn't sure he *actually* experienced true emotions. I'd yet to see them.

He had answered my last question quietly, with feeling.

After a few moments of careful breathing, I said, "So, you didn't use the tech phone because you thought I was heartless enough to make you spend the night in your craft on the roof next door?"

"Yes."

I didn't tell him I'd considered it. He already knew. "Well, you're here. I let you in when I could've left you to rot on my balcony, shivering in the rain, likely to blow yourself up. And you're clean"—*almost naked*—"and in my state-of-the-art sleeping pod from seventy-ish years ago, with programmable features like an ultraviolet automated wake-up. I don't think that qualifies as heartless."

"I didn't say heartless. You did. I simply said you would've said no."

"You not sharing your past makes me uneasy. That's why I would've said no."

"I know."

"You don't know everything."

"That's true."

"Dammit, Case. Quit doing that. You're being agreeable but evasive. It's something you're very skilled at, but it gets us nowhere."

"Where are we trying to get?"

I paused, my palms wet, my fingers twisted, pockets of sweat in the creases. I pulled my hands apart. He'd spoken quietly, which distracted me. "To trust," I replied firmly, chastising my heart for being too erratic, slowing down only to speed up again a second later.

Trust was something I valued above most everything else.

Without trust, there was nothing. Our world was volatile and harsh. If you couldn't count on the person who was supposed to have your back, there was no one.

"Trust."

"Yep," I replied. "After trust, everything else falls into place."

"And in order to earn that, in your opinion, I have to expose every single detail about my past?" His voice held resentment mixed with sadness.

"No…not exactly," I hedged.

"You require more than I can give. I think that means we're at an impasse," he said.

I pondered. "We might be. Though trust can also be earned through actions, as well, which is why you're here and not out on my balcony or shot through the temple with my Gem." I paused. "But even though your actions in the past have gained you access to the group, it's not enough for me. There are too many missing links with you, too many dark corners I can't see around. Too many times you had me second-guessing your motive and then backed it up with a weak excuse." This conversation was slowly morphing into something else, but I wasn't sure exactly what.

"Then I guess I'll have to work a little harder to convince you."

"I guess you will." I blew out a long breath, suddenly exhausted by absolutely everything. "Good night, Case."

He didn't answer. A short time later, rhythmic breathing filtered through the room, the shallow intake and outtake of breaths. The bastard had fallen asleep before I could.

I lay awake for a long time, trying to figure out what our words had meant.

Chapter 6

I awoke with a start, which was normal. It took me a moment to get my bearings, and when I did, I was pissed off. My muscles were tight, my back sore, my hands cramped from clutching my guns for ten hours straight.

Hardly the night of relaxation I'd intended.

That might be the lesson in itself. Never let your guard down, and never pretend you have downtime.

The lid to my sleeping pod was open. I hadn't awoken with a simulated sunrise, but I needed UV. Case walked out of the waste room as I reached up to close the top. He was fully dressed, his face tinted pink.

It seemed someone had enjoyed the sim-sunrise wakeup.

"I'll be out in twenty," I grumbled. "Then I'll be ready to go in ten. I have a battery pack you can borrow for your craft. It's on the wall. It should be enough to get you back to the barracks for a refill." I shut the lid before he had a chance to respond. It'd been careless of him not to make sure Seven was recharged once we'd arrived back in the city. His situation could've been a lot worse.

Twenty minutes went by too quickly, especially with the delicious light tingling and energizing my skin, but at least my muscles were loose and pliant now. The heat felt incredibly good. I stretched within the confines of the pod, curling my toes, bending my elbows over my head. I didn't usually take my dose of UV with so few clothes on, so it felt extra nice. Any more than twenty minutes and I would've burned. I knew my limits.

Once out of the pod, I headed to the waste room, relieved Case was in the living area. I heard him moving around, likely making something to eat. We were supposed to be at the Emporium soon. The fact that nobody had reached out on a tech phone was good. It meant there hadn't been any trouble overnight.

Dressing quickly, I grabbed my weapons and headed to the other room.

My wall screen was on, and the wispy clouds drifted over a deep blue background. Hot water had been left on the counter, an open bag of protein flakes next to it. I dumped the water in without comment and ate my meal, positioning myself against the counter, facing Case, but not looking at him.

It was nice that everyone in the room was fully dressed.

In between bites, I said, "Everything is tasteless since we had Walt's printed food. I miss his cupcakes. I'm pretty sure they'll always be my favorite food, no matter what happens or how many recipes I try." I was pretty sure my dreams last night revolved around the flavor and consistency of that first cupcake, and not at all about Case without his shirt on.

The outskirt was seated on the bench, a pack of batteries he'd taken from the wall in his hand. "There's no joy in eating anymore."

"Exactly." I finished the bag, crumpled it up, and threw it in my grinder, punching the button. "But, honestly, did it ever hold any pleasure?" I went into the hallway, placing my finger on the upper right quadrant of my closet, where I kept my stash of extra weapons, my jacket, and my vest.

I slid on the shell first, then the vest, which fit me perfectly. My seamstress had outdone herself. I'd have to remember to give her some extra coin the next time I saw her and find Lockland something for his trouble.

Case walked up behind me, positioning his trench over his shoulders. He had the batteries. "I think one pack is enough," he said.

I nodded as I zipped up my clothing, patting the pockets to make sure everything was in place. "That should be plenty. To get it hooked up, take the wires here—" My bare hand brushed his, and I snapped it back automatically. Then, trying to cover up my odd behavior, I decided to grab the entire thing out of his hand. "I'll just show you when we get there." I shoved the battery pack into a pocket, then slid on my gloves. "We can fly Seven to the Emporium together. Luce is parked a few buildings away, and it'll take me an hour to get to her, so this works better." I started for the door. After a second, I realized Case wasn't following. Glancing over my shoulder, I asked, "What?"

He shook his head slowly, his mouth quirking up on one side in amusement. "Nothing."

"Good. Let's go." I pulled open the door after casually engaging the heat sensor and headed out. Instead of my usual route, which would've taken us to a hatch that led to the roof at the end of the hallway, I stopped in front of the door that went to the balcony. The same one Case had come through last night.

I was certain no one else had tried to breach it last night, as my alarms would've sounded, not to mention the explosions. But checking was always advisable. It kept you alive. I placed my ear to the door. Case stood to my right, still grinning.

"Honestly, what?" I asked. "By the way, you look like a different person when you're smiling. I'm not used to it. It's making me uneasy, like you might have a seizure or something. What exactly do you find so amusing?"

"I was just imagining you wearing that outfit from last night."

"My pajamas?" I narrowed my gaze. "You found them funny?"

"They didn't exactly look…formidable."

"I wasn't trying to be formidable." I crossed my

arms, bracing a shoulder against the wall. "I was trying to relax. Something I do less than one single time per year. And I can't believe I have to point this out, but I wasn't the only one who wasn't dressed for battle last night. Perhaps you'd like to strip down for the meeting today? Maybe take a shirt off and relax? I'm sure the crew at the Emporium would appreciate the visual of your naked chest." I didn't wait for him to answer. Instead, I yanked the door open with a little more force than necessary. It snapped Case in the forehead midswing. "Whoops," I said. "Sorry about that." *Not sorry.*

I was down the corridor before Case caught up, rubbing his head.

My hand popped the latch quickly, my back to the outskirt as I disarmed the bomb inside. Out on the balcony, I sidestepped my other traps and grabbed the cable from where Case had attached it to the wall after he'd swung over last night.

Climbing up on the railing, I turned to Case. "See you on the other side. Try not to blow yourself up while I'm gone." I stuck my foot in the loop and leaped off. The view from fifty stories up could mess with your brain. It was best not to look down. I'd been scaling buildings my entire life, so it didn't register.

This particular swing was mounted on the building I was heading toward, meaning, if left to swing on its own, it would land there.

I crossed the railing no problem, arching my back to land easily on the ground, my gloves trailing down the cable, keeping it in my grasp once I landed. In one motion, I turned toward Case on the other side, twenty meters away. I contemplated not tossing the cable back and just taking Seven and leaving without him. After all, I had the battery pack with me, and the outskirt had irritated me, making me feel things that I wasn't interested in feeling.

It would be easier if he just left altogether. Or if I did.

He saw my hesitation and slowly shook his head.

"Damn," I muttered. "If I don't send this back, the bastard will just show up unannounced again." I lifted the cable behind my head and lobbed it toward him, giving it a strong sendoff. Then I headed through the residence.

If he didn't catch it, not my fault.

This building was unstable at best, its structure almost completely shot. I made my way up to the roof by way of a rickety stairway. It listed in the breeze, creaking and tottering as I took the steps two at a time.

The new battery pack took a few minutes to attach, and I was sliding out from under Seven when Case finally made it to the roof. He was a little out of breath. I stood, clapping my hands off, grinning. "Took you more than one try?"

Case's expression changed as his eyes landed somewhere over my shoulder, his face going slack as he dove for me. One arm curled around my waist as he yanked us down to the ground, rolling under a chunk of metal attached to a lookout shack I'd crafted long ago so I could see the roof of my residence.

We crashed to a stop, and before I could say anything, he whispered, "UAC."

The air had been completely knocked out of my lungs on impact, and I struggled to catch my breath. Once it leveled out, I whispered, "What direction was it moving?"

"It was coming up over the top of the building."

We lay still for a few more seconds. "Our location is already compromised," I pointed out. "Seven is sitting right there, out in the open. I think we should make a run for it. So far, the UACs have only been monitoring the situation. None of them have engaged." I tried to move, but Case was in the way, his arm still caught beneath me. I began to untangle myself from him by lifting up my back and shoving at his shoulder. "Let's go. I don't hear anything."

"These don't make much noise," he whispered, accommodating me by finally easing his arm out from under my waist.

"How do you know?" I strained, trying to listen. "Have you seen one up close before?" I'd gotten only a glimpse of one from a distance, not close enough to hear anything.

"Yes," he said, his voice gruff.

"If this one has laser capacity, and they shoot at us, they declare war," I murmured. "They won't do that until they assess the threat and figure out who we are and what we know. There's low risk of going into battle right now." That was my best guess anyway. "We get in Seven and try to lose them. It's the only option we have. We can't just stay here, huddled under the shack."

After a moment, Case responded with a reluctant, "Fine, but we go fast, and I'm flying."

I didn't argue.

He rolled out first, lofting the pilot-side door. I jumped in, sliding across to the passenger seat, shoving my arms through the shoulder harness as Case roared Seven to life, launching us off the ground.

"Is it following?" I craned my head around to glance out the rear window. At first, I didn't spot anything, then I saw it darting around quickly as it pursued us. Its movements were as fluid side to side as they were up and down. I'd never seen anything like it. I turned to Case. "How is that thing powered? And how come you knew it doesn't make any noise?"

Case was busy flying, taking turn after turn, achieving angles I hadn't witnessed him do before, making me thankful I'd strapped in as I clutched the side of the craft to keep myself stable. "I've seen one up close before," he finally said. "Once when Dixon and I were in the city years ago. We lost it, but it took some time."

"Was it after you specifically?" I asked.

"Yes."

"If this UAC belongs to the Bureau of Truth, that means they wanted you and Dixon and you've had run-ins with them before?"

"Yes."

I swore.

There was so much we didn't know about this outskirt, and he had patently refused to answer my questions last night. "You've got some explaining to do, as usual. If we manage to lose this thing, we have to get out of town and head to the barracks. We can't stay in the city. I'm alerting the crew and telling them to meet us there."

Case tossed me a surprised look.

"The Bureau of Truth clearly recognizes this craft," I said, "which you just confirmed. We can't risk luring that thing to the Emporium, so we lose it and head out to the barracks." He didn't comment. "What's it going to be, Case? Are you with us or against us? The UAC never chased Lockland like this, it only observed him. It found you—or Seven—and now it's on our trail and it's not going to stop. We have no choice but to get out of town. After that, you owe all of us a *detailed* explanation of how it recognized your craft." After a long, silent pause, I huffed, "Make up your mind, Case."

"Fine. We go to the barracks."

Chapter 7

"Jerry, it's Ella," I said into the tech phone. "Change of plans. Can't make it to Mary's." I braced myself against the side of the craft as Case made a 180-degree turn, then shot through a sheared gap in a building.

The UAC was ever present. We'd been trying to outrun it for the last fifteen minutes with no luck.

Lockland's voice came over the airwaves a second later. "No problem. How about seventh?" He was suggesting we meet in Government Square, under the cover of picking up our overdue protein cakes that we didn't need anymore, because thanks to Case and the stockpile at the barracks, we had plenty to eat.

Meeting out in the open often held an appeal, as it lent us the image of carrying on in a normal capacity without arousing suspicion.

But that wasn't what I had in mind.

I had to be careful in my response, assuming the Bureau of Truth was monitoring all channels and bandwidths. If they knew enough about us to find our residences, then they probably knew our handles. Voice-recognition software still existed—or so I'd heard. A government group like this one would have access to things we didn't know about.

"No, actually, I can't make it at all. I'm sick." My head bounced off the back of the seat as Case engaged the hydro-boost. It was a good plan, until I saw he was heading into the clouds, which was one of my least-favorite places to be. At this rate, we'd be out of the city and out of radio communication quickly. "If you could bring a jug of aminos to my residence, that will help me feel better. I'm parched, too." My mind raced, coming up with something on the spot. "I'm having some protein cakes delivered, but they won't arrive for another fifteen or twenty minutes." I was essentially telling them that I needed backup and we were heading twenty minutes away, near water, and they needed to leave immediately.

Now I had to let them know how to find us.

They already knew the general area of the barracks from my previous descriptions, but since we didn't have exact coordinates or maps for such a thing, it'd been impossible for me to tell them exactly where it was. But, ultimately, if they headed east of the city and followed the sea, I could devise a signal that would catch their attention. A fire would work.

"Will do," Lockland answered, his voice clipped to let me know he understood.

I had only moments before we lost the connection.

"My fever is heating up. Have to go—" The phone went dead.

"Do you think they got it?" Case asked.

"Yes." We'd been up in the clouds for a few minutes, the boost beginning to slow. "Once we arrive at the barracks, we're going to light a fire on the roof." I glanced behind us. "Did you lose the UAC?"

"Too soon to tell," Case answered as he depressed a button on the dash and all the radio signals the craft emitted went dead. "But that thing won't be able to see through clouds, so if I keep changing direction, we should be fine."

"This would be an excellent time to have Maisie with us," I said. "That status reader comes in handy in these situations." I squinted out the back window, trying not to worry about being in the clouds. "Why are we still up here? You should've effectively lost that thing when you hydro-boosted. Why wasn't that enough?"

"It boosted along with us," he growled.

"Its body is too small," I argued, slightly shocked by his answer. "Where would it house a hydrogen canister?" The boost we'd used came from a reaction inside a specialized canister that forced the explosion outward, rocketing us forward. It needed to be fairly large to exert that much energy.

Case shook his head. "It utilizes different technology."

I turned to him, exasperated. "How do you know *that*?"

He was quiet.

I was irritated.

He began our descent out of the clouds. I couldn't tell which direction we were headed, and with the dash dark, there was no way to know until we had a visual. After a long exhale, Case finally replied, "Dixon was a member of the Bureau of Truth—a former member. That's how I know."

I slumped back in my seat, my eyelids sliding shut, a single index finger coming to rest at my temple, beginning to move in a slow, rhythmic circle. "Case." I kept my head down, not wanting to look at him. I was sick of the game. "When exactly were you planning on sharing that detail with us? We talked in depth about the Bureau of Truth in Bender's shop when we returned from the South. That would've been an excellent time. Or how about when Lockland explained he was being monitored by the very same UAC that just gave us chase? Or when we were trying to figure out who controls the government building that houses the only working medi-pod that can help Mary and all the other seekers? Or, lastly, last night when we were talking? Any one of those times would've been good enough, although anything that came after our debriefing back in town would've been considered late, but *possibly* forgivable. This is just...so typical."

Case dropped us completely out of the vapor, giving us our first glimpse of the horizon. We were a lot farther out than I'd anticipated. The city was nothing more than a speck in the distance behind us.

Luckily, nothing seemed to be following us—at least nothing I could see.

In front, the sea was roaring up fast. Case had managed to aim Seven in the exact right direction. Why was I surprised? Nothing would ever surprise me about this man ever again. He was an outskirt, blood and bone.

"It's not like that," he finally said.

"Not like what?" My tone was steeped in resentment. "You keep secrets—and continue to keep them—even when they're detrimental to the safety of this group. As soon as Lockland and Bender find out that the Bureau of Truth is following us to track you down, and you didn't say anything about it, you're out." I continued to rub my temple. At this point, a tension headache was imminent. "And, you know, if I were you, I wouldn't fight it. Kicking you out without physical harm is a gift. The only reason they won't retaliate is because you sav—*helped*—me in the past. Honestly, it's better this way—"

"Dixon was in the group, not me." Case was angry. His molars ground together as he spoke. Good. "When I flew this craft back to the city, they must've noticed. I didn't know until ten minutes ago that it was going to be an issue, or I would've said something."

I shook my head, dropping my hand. "Bullshit. If you had details about the Bureau of Truth—anything Dixon had told you—you should've shared them, or at least warned us. They control the medi-pod we need, and we're about to launch ourselves into a war with them, yet you stayed quiet. There's no excuse for that."

"There is."

"What?" I turned to give him my full attention.

"Death to anyone who knows their secret." He paused, allowing time for that to sink in. It didn't penetrate as deeply as he apparently thought it would, but I let him continue. "That's why Dixon didn't enlighten me with specifics about the agency. All I know is, he was part of the group and later defected. The UAC chased us once while we were in the city, but it wasn't an issue. He never shared any details because he didn't want to put my life at risk."

I made a noise in the back of my throat, a quick exhale that turned into a snort. "The only way your life would've ended was if they'd captured you," I stated. "And if that had happened, chances are you would've died anyway. But even that information alone—that it would be a death sentence to talk about them—would've been helpful to us." The roiling waves came into sharp focus as Case angled Seven to the right, hugging the coast. "The problem is you like keeping secrets. And, honestly, that's not always a bad thing. But that means you work alone. I don't think it's possible for you to let your guard down. Being part of a group dynamic means you forfeit your secrets for the sake of everyone else. You can't handle that."

"I can."

"You can't."

"You kept your E-unit secret," he challenged.

"My E-unit was not a direct threat to anyone. But it's a threat to them now that they know about it. If they were captured and given Babble, they would be penalized for even having the knowledge of its existence and not telling the government."

"I've been taught differently than you," he argued. "I've learned to keep everything close unless it's absolutely necessary."

"By saying that, you're proving my point," I answered. "The information you kept to yourself was pertinent to the group two days ago, yet you didn't share. I think we can agree that *absolutely necessary* means something different to you than it does to me."

"No." He was being obstinate. "It wasn't necessary until now."

"I give up. I'm tired of arguing with you. We'll see what the others say when they arrive." I arched an eyebrow in his direction. "But if it was up to me, you'd be out. Lockland, Bender, and Darby each get a vote. The good thing about the barracks being so far out is you have time to get your story straight while we light the fire."

Up ahead, the landmarks I'd come to recognize came into view. One was a copse of trees shaped like a semicircle. Case veered, skimming over the tops of the dead pines, instead of angling out toward the sea. The barracks was only accessible by coming in from the west over the ocean.

Before I could ask him what he was doing, he offered, "I'm not taking any chances. The UAC or whoever is manning it doesn't know where we are now, but if it finds the barracks, we risk losing too much." He continued down the coast for another five minutes and then began a sharp descent, landing behind a small sand dune ninety meters from the crashing sea.

Once we were down and the props were off, I made an attempt to open the door, then thought better of it. There wasn't anywhere to go. I sat back in my seat, drawing one leg up. "How long are we going to wait?"

"Ten minutes," he answered.

"We can't see over the hill in front of us," I said. "The only way we'll see anything from this position is if it flies over our heads."

"That's the idea," Case replied. "If it's in close pursuit, we want to take it by surprise. I don't think there's any way it could track us here, especially after the boost, but they'll stay on the hunt for several kilometers in every direction from where they lost us. I was careful to go south before I headed east."

"You're extremely skilled when it comes to navigating," I admitted. "You just suck at a lot of the other stuff." I sighed.

"No, I just choose to do things differently than you do."

I angled my head toward him, keeping it firmly against the seat. "I don't know how many times I can keep saying this, but if you choose to be part of a crew, the collective comes before the individual. It's not a concept you're capable of grasping." He gave me a look, anger mixed with a touch of indignation. I gave him a look right back that conveyed exactly how I felt about having to have this conversation again. "What's it going to take to get you to admit that sharing information you had about the Bureau of Truth was relevant and could've helped us? Please enlighten me."

He sat, contemplative for a while, neither of us speaking.

Then he leaned up and switched on the props. "You're right. I should've shared."

"Damn right you should've." I was robbed of taking a greater amount of pleasure in the outskirt's admission, because we'd sat so long my brain had turned to worrying about my crew getting out here safely without being detected. Because that's what you did when you were part of a group. You worried about them.

I desperately hoped Daze wasn't too freaked out. The kid and I hadn't been separated since the day I saved him from plunging to his death on the gorge. I knew he was worried about me.

Case lifted us up and over the dune, hugging the ground, skimming back up the coast toward the barracks. After a moment, he said, "There's a hatch inside the battery room. We can use that to climb out on the roof. We start the fire a ways away. We can't leave any crafts out in the open, especially if the UAC decides to go farther afield searching for us. Once they land, we'll figure out where to go, and I'll shuttle them back and forth."

"Sounds good," I said, still distracted. "It'll take some time to do that, but it'll be worth it to keep the barracks secure." If the government found out this place existed, they'd fight us with everything they had to take it. It was too valuable.

Case set us down smoothly in the hollowed-out parking spot at the entry of the barracks. After he shut the props down, he turned to me. "I didn't mean to withhold information from the group. I was trying to keep everyone safe."

I lofted the door, placing a foot on the ground, the thunderous waves almost drowning out my response. "You can apologize to the others when they get here, but I have no idea if it will be enough."

Chapter 8

"We're letting him off the hook, just like that?" I tried to keep my voice down and hold back the growl that was forming, but it proved beyond my talents. "He kept vital information from us! He shouldn't get a pass."

We were all gathered in the seating area of the barracks. Lockland, Bender, Darby, and Daze had arrived in two crafts not long after Case and I had started the fire half a kilometer away, using a bunch of dead tree branches and some accelerant we'd found inside. They'd flown an additional two kilometers to park, and Case had followed, bringing them back to the barracks in two trips, just like we'd planned.

"You heard him," Bender said, not bothering to keep *his* growl concealed. "The only information Case had was that they are dangerous. We already knew that."

"Yeah, and that Dixon was a former member," I said. "And the Bureau of Truth could identify Dixon's old craft, because they'd already gone after them before, because they were pissed off that he was a defector. Just by flying in the city, Case posed a threat to us. He could've at least given us the courtesy of a warning. Case is too used to working solo. Withholding information could get us killed, and everyone here knows it." I tried to shift my body to the side, but I ran into Daze, who had positioned himself at my hip pretty much since the moment he'd arrived.

"We understand what you're saying, and we agree," Lockland said. It certainly wasn't coming across that way. "It's going to take the outskirt time to adjust to working in a group."

"And we're allowing for that these days?" I said. "Without any stipulations or penalties? We've never granted anyone that amount of leeway—*ever*." There had been a few people over the years who had joined our crew briefly. We'd ultimately let them go due to trust issues, or the fact that they hadn't been smart enough to keep themselves alive, let alone the rest of us.

"I remember when I first joined," Darby said. "I was so nervous you guys weren't going to accept me. I knew I couldn't afford to mess anything up, so I was extremely careful."

I gestured at Darby, who sat across the tech table from me. "See? Darby, the gentlest and most trusting among us, knew he couldn't screw up. And he was right not to, because we don't give second and third chances." I directed my next question at Darby. "Did you ever even *think* about keeping anything of value from us? Or lying?"

Before he could answer, Lockland stood, making his way out and around the seating area. "I think the question here is more about your relationship with Case," he said, "than it is about his relationship with us, or keeping things from us as a group."

"What the hell is that supposed to mean?" I asked, following him.

He stopped by the cooling unit. "I'm just saying that you two spend the most time together. And that means he has a greater number of hours to piss you off. Yeah, he didn't tell us that one of his old acquaintances worked for the Bureau of Truth, but he didn't have any other pertinent information to share, other than they will kill anyone who knows their secret, which is not hard to infer, given the circumstances we're finding ourselves in now." Lockland took out a jug of water and shut the door. I took a cup out of the cabinet and handed it to him. "If he'd kept vital things from us, that would definitely be an issue. But as it stands, the info's not that detrimental."

"Dixon was more than an acquaintance," I argued, leaning against the counter, crossing my arms. "He was a powerful mentor who we just found out was a former government official gone rogue. You can't forget that Dixon killed an entire militia by himself. I remember Case telling me he had connections in the city. We also have no idea if Case is keeping anything else from us, because he won't say one way or another.

That's the main problem here. He has no reason to share his information with us, and now you're deciding it's not worth giving him one."

Case was out spreading the ashes from the fire, making sure they were covered with a layer of sand. He'd left right after he'd confessed to the group that he'd omitted key details about the Bureau of Truth, Dixon, and his craft being recognized and apologized for leaving them out in the first place.

I had to admit, he'd sounded contrite. But you never knew with the outskirt. It still made me uncomfortable not knowing his angle, because he definitely had an angle.

"Case is going to be back soon," Darby said, entering the eating area, Daze trailing after. Darby picked up a bag of dried flakes and handed one to the kid. "We have to decide what we're going to do. I'm kind of in agreement with Holly on this. I mean, we should at least give him some kind of parameters to follow in the future, and if he breaks those, he's out. He didn't do anything terrible this time, he just omitted some stuff. We could let him off with a warning, but I think it'd be a mistake to let it go without future consequence."

"Thanks, Darb," I said, pouring a cup of water to heat up with the whisk. We were all hungry.

"Fine." Bender joined us, pulling open the cooling unit and grabbing out a jug of aminos. I made a face. Aminos were nasty fresh. I couldn't imagine what old aminos tasted like. He took a long swallow, then dragged his forearm over his mouth. He didn't immediately retch, so that was an encouraging sign. "We give him one more chance to spill everything he knows, and if we find out later that he omitted anything major, he's gone. I will personally shove him out."

Shove him out meant Case's ousting would be physical. He'd be required to leave the city for good under the threat of death. The method for shoving someone out could be any number of things, the least of which being Bender's fists.

That kind of threat would make many people quake, but it wouldn't do a damn thing to affect Case or his choices. The outskirt wasn't afraid of going head-to-head with Bender, or likely anything we could do to him physically.

The threat of being shoved out wasn't enough.

"That's a good start," I said. "But we have to throw in something that matters. He doesn't care about himself. I say, if he betrays us, we go after his family." If I'd learned anything about him, I'd learned that family was deeply important to him. The Sun Optimist group had kept him alive and had given him a reason to live. He owed them. "We don't kill them, but they suffer." Darby gave me a look like I'd disappointed him. "What? It's the only way he'll take us seriously, and I want to be done with this once and for all. No more wondering if Case could've helped us and chose not to for his own sake, or if he's planning on hedging his bets and siding with the Bureau of Truth if things start to get risky." I glanced around at my crew, each with a bag of warmed-up-enough protein mush in hand. "It seems we have some selective memories here. Case played both sides up until he shot Hutch. Yet we let him stay anyway, because he was an asset moving forward. And I fully admit he was helpful down South. I think he's trying to be a team player, but I'm not willing to risk my family on this outskirt, and dammit, none of you should either."

"I'm with Holly." Daze shoveled in a mouthful of food. "I think Case is nice and all, but he has to prove himself before we can trust him."

I tossed an arm across the kid's shoulders. I could easily reach him, because he'd sidled up to me again. The separation last night, followed by evacuating the city quickly, had gotten to him, even though he hadn't uttered a word about it. "That he does."

"Just like me," he said, glancing up, his eyes a little glossy. "I still have to earn your trust. I did a bad thing, even though I didn't mean to. If I had family, you could go after them. I'm working really hard not to mess up again."

My heart clenched as it gave an irregular beat. I was saved from responding by Maisie, who said from Daze's pocket, "Trust is the union of belief in something by two or more people. Trust is considered sacred in many cultures. Trust is—"

"Stop, Maisie," Lockland said, setting down his now empty bag of food. "It's done. We threaten his family, and we mean it. I'll tell him when he comes in."

I nodded. "You don't have to bother," I said. "I'm

certain he still has amplifiers set up and is listening right now. That's the way he operates. He's protecting himself, which he should be allowed to do—up to a point."

Bender glanced around the large space, taking another swig of aminos. "This is military from way back, not just militia." The militia had popped up after the dark days as a necessity, first to aid the people and help rebuild—or rather, scavenge and repurpose. Then to act as guardians and gatekeepers for the government.

"Yes," I said. "It's definitely military. The old insignias are stamped all over the crates. I haven't had much time to snoop around, but it's amazing that nobody found this place before now. If the government knew these kinds of supplies existed, in this much excess, they'd be all over this area."

Lockland walked toward the row of sleeping pods. They were stacked two high and rolled out seamlessly. The fronts of the pods were firmly connected to the wall to provide structure. "Once Case returns," Lockland said, "we formulate a plan to infiltrate the Bureau of Truth. Pursuing you was an act of aggression we can't ignore. We strike soon, before everyone gets too comfortable. Not to mention, Walt and the others down South are waiting for us to return, and Mary needs help. We can't waste any time."

I addressed Darby, who was in the process of opening another bag of protein flakes. "Speaking of Mary, did you give her Plush like we talked about?"

"Yes," Darby answered. "It calmed her down immediately. I gave Ned a small dart to give her if she gets bad again. But Lockland's right, we're running out of time. We have to find that medi-pod, and if it's not working, I have to start trying to build a replica. I'm not at all certain I can achieve it, but I have to try."

I nodded. "I agree."

Lockland came toward us. "Right before we left the city, I received news about the mover drone. My source got back to me early this morning. He thinks those in charge of Port Station will be up for a trade, but they want to meet face-to-face."

I frowned. "They've never requested a personal meeting before, have they? That sounds like the markings of a trap to me."

Lockland pierced me with his gaze. "It does. I won't go in alone. It's a little unusual, but I've never offered them a trade before either. I've only given them coin and salvaged goods as bribes. So the ask is somewhat warranted, but I'll proceed with caution."

"Does your guy have much power in the group?" I asked. Lockland didn't divulge his sources.

Lockland shrugged. "A decent amount. But what's more important is that he has the ear of the one who's in charge, someone they call Billy. With your E-unit, they'd be able to make several hundred bombs, and by the sounds of it, they want to avoid anything like Tandor and his group happening again." Tandor had infiltrated Port Station and taken it over, which had been a large feat, and he'd done it without us knowing.

"What are the chances they'll align themselves with us?" Bender asked, heading to the two couches on either side of the tech table, Lockland following.

"I think there's a high likelihood," Lockland replied as he took a seat. "That's the end result I'm hoping for. But as it stands, I'm going to have to meet with him before we act against the Bureau of Truth. With Port Station's backing, we'll be bolstered, which will help."

I tossed away my bag of food and made my way over to the seating area.

Case chose that moment to exit the room that held the batteries, coming from the roof. He moved forward, clapping off his hands, a spray of sand sprinkling the ground.

He stopped in front of me, Daze at my side.

"Did you overhear our discussion?" I asked, my face set, daring him to deny he had amplifiers.

"Yes," he answered, unmoved.

"Good, then you know what's at stake," I said. "We're giving you one last chance to come clean with everything you know—and I mean *everything*. After that, if we find out you've been holding back for any reason, we're targeting the last of your sustainee siblings, starting with Wendra." I really only knew about two of his siblings, Freedom and Wendra, and then there were all of Freedom's wives and children. "Do you agree to our terms?"

He gave me a hard look, the corners of his eyes tightening. "Yes."

Chapter 9

"And where do you think these mysterious files might be located?" I was positioned with my shoulder against one of the giant pillars. Case had just finished telling us everything he knew about Dixon, which wasn't much, other than he was an ex-government-agent-turned-militia-man and *might* have kept diaries or some kind of records about his dealings. Case hadn't bothered to try to find them once Dixon had died. Why was anyone's guess.

Without a doubt, Case was still holding back. But was the nature of what he'd omitted essential to us or just personal?

"I have no idea where Dixon kept his personal journals," Case said as he rose from the couch, where he'd relayed his story, sans any emotion. "I told you, I'm not even sure anything exists. Dixon had a few contacts he kept in touch with in the city, but I never knew their names, never saw them, and have no idea if they were government or not. Dixon never said either way. If you knew Dixon, you'd understand that he didn't share and didn't tolerate probing questions."

"Dixon had a vendetta against other militias," I pointed out, shoving off from the pillar. "He kept contacts in the city. When he came to your militia and killed everyone, you left with him. And you never bothered to ask why he took down an entire troop? Logically, you were owed an explanation, even if he didn't choose to elaborate."

Maisie, who was now located on top of the powered-down tech table, interrupted with, "The definition of a militia is a group of—"

"Stop," I commanded the egg. She ceased immediately. This was the fifth random definition she'd spouted since Daze had taken her out of his pocket. "No more definitions unless we ask, Maisie."

"Okay, Holly," she replied. "I detect intelligent software beneath me. It lacks power, but it can be enabled."

My gaze landed on the tech table. We knew it worked, because we'd used it to charge the pico, but we hadn't taken the time to uncover its other uses. It might be an asset. "Thanks for the information," I told her. We'd learned that praising her encouraged similar behavior. "We'll check it out in a minute." I glanced at Case, who'd stopped in front of me. "We're not done here," I told him. "If you think Dixon kept information about his past in the form of journals, including what he was up to and who he was conspiring with, you must—at the very least—be able to give an educated guess about where he would've hidden them. Where did you spend the most time?"

Lockland was reclining on one of the couches. Bender turned in his seat to face us. Both shot expectant looks at Case. They weren't letting him off the hook this time. They knew, just as much as I did, that he was still withholding.

What the outskirt had chosen to share had barely taken ten minutes, and he and Dixon had been together for years. Case was risking a lot by not divulging more.

"In the year prior to his death, we were headquartered here," Case answered tightly. He was visibly uncomfortable, which piqued my attention.

"When you moved from place to place, did you take everything?" I prodded. "Or did you leave things behind?"

"We took our essentials and personal items," he said.

Lockland stood, making his way toward us. "Did this become your headquarters so you could be close to the city? Did Dixon have regular meetings in the city once he arrived?"

Case nodded, his eyes locked on the ground. "He had meetings fairly regularly, but not always in the city."

If not in the city, then where?

It was odd, since there wasn't anything around here, which meant Dixon likely traveled South.

I shot Case a disgruntled look. "You lived with the man for years, he left regularly, and you don't know where he went?" My voice couldn't have conveyed any more disdain. "You never thought to ask him?"

Bender came to stand by me, crossing his brawny arms in front of him, his feet spread as he confronted Case. "You're leaving something major out, aren't you? You weren't partners, were you? He wasn't your mentor or your savior—your relationship was something else entirely."

My brows furrowed as I glanced at Bender. His face was set, no hint of a growl in his words. I contemplated what he'd said as my gaze landed back on Case, who would not meet my eyes. Then it all came tumbling together. "You were his prisoner." I tried to keep the dismay out of my voice, because Case was so...*capable.* But Bender was right. It was the only thing that made any sense. Case had no real information to share, and there had to be a logical explanation. "Were you...were you...did he keep you to..." I stammered, not able to finish the sentence. There was a highly likely chance that a man like Dixon would save someone like Case so he could use him whenever he wanted.

Case's face clouded with anger as he finally raised his head. "No, I wasn't his sex slave." His voice was dead, void of any emotion. "I would've killed him for that."

"Then why—"

Before I could get the rest out, Case turned and stalked toward the back of the room, disappearing through the door.

"Let him go," Lockland said. "He's going to need some time. We just forced something out of him he never wanted known to the world."

Bender ran a hand over his face as we all moved toward the seating area. "That is seriously fucked up. This guy Dixon comes in and saves him from one bad situation, kills his tormentors, only to hold him hostage for years. Maybe he had savior emotional bullshit mixed in with some hero worship. Otherwise, he would've killed the bastard and been done with it. That's what I would've done."

My eyes tracked to the back of the room. "Damn. It explains a lot." So much. "How do we know Case didn't kill him? I bet my coin he did, and that asshole deserved it." Now that we had the missing piece, which finally explained Case's reluctance to share what he knew about Dixon, things began to make sense. I was ultimately sad to find out the truth, but I was relieved to finally have answers.

Lockland sat forward, bracing his elbows on his thighs. "Keep in mind that he can hear everything we're saying."

"Yeah, about that," I said. "Listening in on us has to end immediately."

"It will," Lockland said. "But we can't forget we're in his space, not the other way around."

"Man, he's had a rough life," Darby muttered. "I think we should cut him some slack in light of this new information."

"I understand the emotional response," I said. I felt

it, too. It messed with my mind in ways I couldn't fully comprehend at the moment. "But we still don't know this outskirt well enough to excuse all of his prior behavior." Yet. I sighed as I ran a hand through my hair, which was still semiclean, since I'd been in the stall last night. It was a little strange to be able to get my fingers through it.

"I don't mean give him a break, as in, we drop all the rules he has to follow," Darby said. "I'm talking about letting him have some breathing room alone."

"We can do that," I agreed. "As soon as we figure out a plan, we're out of here." I was willing to give Case as much time as he needed.

"The first thing on the agenda is Bender and I heading to Port Station," Lockland said. "After that, we figure out the best way to breach the government building. We don't head back to the city until that's done."

"It would be helpful if we had Dixon's notes," I said. "He worked for the bureau. He had to have detailed some things to keep track of his connections. If this is where he and Case stayed for the last year, a journal or tablet, by rights, should be here somewhere."

Daze hopped up from his place next to me. "If it's here, I bet I can find it. I found all those protein flakes when I went looking before. I don't remember seeing any journals, but I wasn't looking for those at the time."

I raised my eyebrows, nodding. "I bet you can, kid. You don't need my permission to start looking." I made an all-encompassing gesture. "Have at it." Daze darted into the middle of the room, disappearing behind a crate. I addressed Lockland. "You and Bender head to Port Station, and Darby and I will try to figure out what the tech table has to offer. I'd be surprised if it doesn't have mapping software or some useful intel about the city."

Lockland nodded. "If we're going to strike the Bureau of Truth, we need to do it when they least expect it." According to Roman's map, the mysterious building that housed the bureau was located in one of the most populated neighborhoods in town. Government Square was where families and law-abiding citizens lived.

"Middle of the day?" I asked. That could backfire on us spectacularly.

"No, I was thinking just after dawn," he said. "They probably aren't expecting us to attack them at home at all, but if they are, they'll figure it'll happen under the cover of blackout. They may relax their guard first thing in the morning."

"We already have an advantage," I said. "They have no idea we're pursuing them because of the medi-pod, so it's unlikely they would think we'd come to them. If they're smart, they'll assume we want to go up against them in a place that's more advantageous to us. Not at their front door. Or basement's door, as it stands."

"We have no idea what they assume yet," he said. "We keep a very low profile moving forward."

"Agreed," I said.

"What we need to do is discuss things with Claire,"

Bender growled. "She's been working her ass off double time to get us information from inside the government about this group. We don't move without talking to her."

"Has anybody heard from her recently?" I asked. I worried about Claire. I couldn't help it, even though I didn't need to, because she had no problem holding her own. She was strong, efficient, and took no shit. But that didn't mean she wasn't vulnerable, especially with the Bureau of Truth looming over her and her small group of loyalists. We'd always been careful to keep our affiliation with her loose, but I'd known her since I was a child. It wouldn't take a brilliant scientist to figure out the connection.

"I heard from her last night," Lockland said. "She mentioned that things are getting tense within the ranks. She has a feeling something's about to happen. She's supposed to get back to me tonight, but if we stay here, we won't get a signal."

"We can fly out later, if needed," I said, relieved there was news. "We don't have to be inside the city limits to get a hold of her."

"Sounds good," Lockland said. "When Case gets back, he can take us to my craft. The meeting in Port Station is set for an hour from now."

I sat back. "Is your source meeting you outside Port Station?"

"Yes," Lockland said. "Our usual location, right past the gate near the old buildings. Bender will be close by, monitoring with an amplifier."

"What does your gut say about this being a setup?" I asked. We couldn't rule it out.

"Higher than ten," he replied. "But I'm eighty-five percent certain they'll be willing to make the trade because they don't want what happened with the takeover of Tandor's men to happen again."

"If that's true," I said, "you'll have bargaining power. If you use my E-unit as leverage, make it count. They will be able to make a lot of bombs, which they could use against us or the city. We don't need that to come back and haunt us later." Port Station was not a well-off city. If the powers that be in Port Station decided to overthrow our main government, we'd technically be aiding them by providing the means to make their own weapons.

"Don't worry, I've got it covered," Lockland said. Behind us, Case came through the doorway. Lockland stood. "The meet shouldn't take longer than two hours."

I nodded. "I'll be monitoring your return."

Chapter 10

Case walked through the front entryway forty-five minutes later, back from dropping Bender and Lockland off, his face drawn. He headed toward the cooling unit without a word. Daze was still searching the area for anything Dixon might've left behind, and Darby had gone to inspect the medi-pod in the back.

The tech table was on, and I was chatting with Maisie. She was issuing me commands, and I was failing to understand them. So far, we'd found only stored topographical maps of the area and locations of government buildings that were likely no longer standing.

It seemed these barracks had been a gathering point for troops in the area. They'd spend a few days here and get their needed supplies and orders before being sent out on their next mission. Nothing overly exciting.

"Interface with the hologram capabilities by placing

the palm of your hand on the bottom right quadrant," Maisie said.

"I've already done that three times," I grumbled. "You keep telling me to do the same thing, and it keeps not working."

Case took a seat across from me, his elbows resting on his thighs, his face blank. His body language indicated that he was in no mood to talk, which I completely ignored.

"Put your hand on the other side," I ordered. "On the bottom right. Maybe the table's turned around, even though the writing is this side up for me."

Case obeyed my command without comment. As soon as his palm hit the table, a large box blinking the word *passcode* flashed on the screen.

I stood and moved to his side of the table, since the lettering had switched to face him, and sat down, but not too close. "Darb, I think we have something," I called. "It's finally showing us something new."

Before I could ask Maisie for help, she said, "Passcode is obscured, but logical. Suggest a rational guess."

"What does she mean by rational?" I asked. "Opposed to irrational?"

Darby scooted next to me, edging me over so I hit Case, who immediately shifted away like I'd fired my laser gun through his thigh. Darby settled in, oblivious. "She means that the military would've used something that new troops coming in would know, something easy."

I turned, raising a single eyebrow. "How in the hell do you understand this status reader so well? It's like you two have a shared brain. Daze is getting there, but when she enters this mode, she makes no sense to me."

Darby chuckled. "It's just standard computerspeak. I've internalized enough data over the years to understand her jargon. It's all constructed similarly. If I was writing her program, I'd use the same words. Daze is smart enough to pick up on it."

Darby was being polite by not calling me out as stupid. Daze knelt next to us. "Smart enough to pick up on what?"

"Apparently," I said, "something that eludes me called computerspeak. Maisie wants us to make a rational guess, versus an irrational guess, at what the passcode to access the table might be."

Maisie said, "Rational constitutes words in the realm of commonality shared by the inhabitants of this location. Irrational would be words chosen at random, meant to confuse."

"I get it now," I grumbled.

Daze began to chirp, "Passcode: troops." When that didn't work, he continued, "Passcode: militia. Passcode: weapons. Passcode: barracks." The word *passcode* kept flashing. Nothing else was happening.

Darby said, "Let's try something more mundane. Passcode: rations. Passcode: sergeant. Passcode: artillery. Passcode: rank."

I glanced around the large space, trying to picture what life would've been like with military personnel all over, what they would've been doing, and how they would've interacted in this space. "What did they call something like this building? There's so much stored here, and we're only occupying one of the levels. There has to be at least ten levels to this place by my count."

Case's voice was low as he intoned, "Passcode: stockade."

The tech table sprang to life.

Small compartments I hadn't even noticed at each corner of the table opened, and small cameras no bigger than my thumb slowly emerged. On cue, they all clicked on, beams of light converging above the tabletop as a man's face began to take shape.

Darby gave a whoosh of excitement, slapping his leg. "It's a 4-D hologram program! At the time, it was brand-new. Almost no one had it. Leave it to the military. The technology makes the images look super lifelike. It's considered 4-D because the images can be manipulated and usually come with sound."

We watched as the man's head solidified, his coloring perfect, his facial expressions clear, the small graying at the edges of his short haircut standing out, as he ordered, "State your mission, rank, and ID, soldier."

Case didn't hesitate. "Mission: intel. Rank: corporal. ID: 76351."

I gaped, my mouth dropping open. "How did you know that number—"

The sergeant interrupted with, "Welcome back, Corporal Harrison. Full access granted." The sergeant's face turned to mist as the tiny pixels wisped apart, coalescing a moment later to create a perfect map of our location. It showed the barracks the way it was before disaster struck.

"His name, rank, and number are etched on the inside of my sleeping pod," Case answered. "I figured he was probably one of the guys stationed here permanently."

I tentatively reached toward the image.

"Go ahead," Darby encouraged. "I think you can manipulate it with your hands. The technology for this was pretty advanced, allowing simple physical interaction with users."

I chuckled. "You sound like Maisie. Pretty soon, we won't be able to tell the two of you apart." Once my finger was close to the outside of the building in the image, the pixels beneath my finger turned red. I tentatively brushed my hand to the right, and the building moved, changing perspective. "Look at all these rooms. I wonder if we can get to them. Do you think they're still stocked?" I moved my finger up and down, side to side, mesmerized by the way the hologram moved. "This is amazing."

Darby scooted forward. "I don't know," he said. "We can certainly try and check it out later. Right now, the most useful thing to us would be a detailed map of the city. This interface is a thousand times better than the one on the pico. I'm not sure if I can integrate the trackers Roman made with this system, but we already know the locations, so if we have access to a detailed map, we can examine the government building we're looking for. The building itself should be old enough to fit this profile. The military had access to every internal schematic of every building or structure built in the last hundred years. Architects and builders were required to download their plans once a building was complete. It was under the guise of keeping people safe, so the government could monitor and access fire alarms, integrated fire-suppression systems, surveillance, and even lockdown capabilities in case of a terrorist attack. But I think they just wanted a legal way to spy on people."

"That sounds about right," I said.

Darby said, "The government was riddled with greed. Deals were made, trillions of dollars exchanged, and in the end the military got what it wanted. It's my belief that, by the time the meteor hit, not one speck of this world was unseen by their eyes."

"They had the ultimate power," Case agreed. "And they didn't give a shit what the lowly people thought."

"Expand map twenty kilometers in every direction," Darby directed the hologram. Nothing happened. He tried again. "Locate nearest city, micro details."

Nothing.

I addressed Case. "You're the one who opened it with the right passcode. It's probably voice sensitive. You ask."

"Open hologram map twenty kilometers north," Case ordered. The pixels dissolved, disintegrating fluidly, joining back together to form a sharp, detailed image of a bustling city. Not only an image—a video.

People were actually moving, crafts flying, trams shuttling inhabitants around.

Breath leaving my body, I sat back in my seat, mesmerized. "It's an old feed." Seeing our ancestors going about their day-to-day business was humbling and a little overwhelming. There were so many of them.

Darby reached out, tentatively touching one of the buildings. The pixels under his fingertips turned red, like they had for me. Not only did the map show the outlines of the buildings themselves, but also fully detailed insides, including furniture, utilities, houseplants, and everything else.

"Are those…are those real people?" Daze asked, his voice barely registering.

"Yes," I said, finally coming out of my shock, leaning forward for a better look. "My guess is this was one of their last active feeds before disaster struck."

"That's as good a guess as any," Darby said. "The hologram software would've utilized multiple live satellites at once, which were knocked out of the sky almost immediately. This has to be the last cached data."

We were witnessing life as it was sixty-plus years ago, right before most of these people perished. It was a disturbing thought.

I couldn't look away.

Everywhere my eyes focused, it was on something unusual and strange. Women wore outfits in which the skin of their arms and legs showed. Their hairstyles were elaborate, many of them piled on top of their heads. Many were wearing large hats. The men wore two-piece outfits, some colorful, some not. Then there were people wearing a mixture of the two, which was fascinating. Hair colors ranged from mellow to vibrant. Crafts floated by at regular intervals, staggered by height depending on which direction they were moving. Public transportation drifted back and forth, mainly vehicles that people had affectionately called people movers, which were large, standing-room-only crafts that stopped dutifully at almost every intersection. Up higher, scrapers were joined by clear skywalks that featured efficiently moving walkways.

Darby slowly slid his finger to the right, taking us farther into the city.

None of us could formulate words, until I finally sputtered, "Do you see how many animals they have?" It struck me as one of the strangest things, never having seen a live animal before. They were everywhere. "They have them hooked to short cables in the streets, and they run freely in the homes. I think our ancestors were animal crazy."

"Yes, most everyone had a pet," Darby said. "They were allowed to take them everywhere. Places called restaurants—where people ordered exotic food—workplaces, homes, schools. They were revered and thought to have soothing qualities. Our ancestors lived high-stress lives. I didn't really understand it before, but seeing their interactions with the animals here, it seems peaceful and happy."

It did.

"I wish some of them had survived," Daze said sadly. "I think I would've liked having a pet."

It was almost too much to take in.

Darby began moving his fingers precisely, dragging the map farther and farther until he found what he was looking for. Then he used his index finger and thumb on each hand to enlarge the space. "This is the government building that Roman marked in his map," he said.

Case and I both moved forward at the same time, our shoulders touching. "This might have been a government building all along," I said. "Look, there's a main desk. The people sitting there are wearing uniforms. If it is, that might help us."

Darby thrust the building upward, dragging our view down below street level to the basement. "I think this is the room that Roman highlighted." He tapped the map, leaving three red dots fading in his wake. "I have the pico with me, and I can double-check later. But see that? Here are the same three entry points shown on the 3-D map." Darby spun the hologram, and sure enough, the room had three entrances. One was up a story, accessed by a set of stairs.

I squinted, pointing to a darkened area nearby. "That looks like a tunnel to me."

Darby dragged the image to the right, and a zoom tunnel popped into view. Dozens of people were riding automated walkways as we watched. It was surreal to see them actually using a place that had mostly been inaccessible for all these years.

Millions of people a day had accessed zoom tunnels to get to the hypertube stations, which housed the magnetic-levitation trains that shuttled them from place to place beneath the city and beyond.

"It is a zoom tunnel," he cautioned, "but there's a high likelihood that this location is no longer usable, either caved in or filled with water."

Daze sputtered excitedly, "Look, that train is going into the airlock. That's so cool." Because mag-lev trains were buoyed by strong magnets and operated in a vacuum, there was no friction, which allowed riders to reach their destinations in minutes, or traverse the entire United States in only a few hours.

"Go back to the room we're trying to get to," I instructed Darby. He slid the map back to the basement. "Now go left a few meters." He did as I asked. "Stop right there." I leaned in closer, bringing my hand up. Darby dropped his and sat back. I enlarged the image myself, grinning. "Do you see that?" My voice was unchecked in its excitement.

"What?" Darby squinted, moving forward again. "I see another zoom tunnel with lots of people waiting for a train."

"That's one of our underground spaces," I said. "I'm sure of it. I know, because we enter from the top. Right here in the maintenance shaft of this building." I tapped my finger, and the hologram blinked red right over our entrance spot. The broken-down building we used had long since been abandoned, but here it looked perfectly sound. "We come down these steps, then crawl through this area." I outlined the route with my finger. "To end up here." I marked it with an X. "It looks like we're lucky that a mag-lev was parked there when the meteor struck."

"It *is* our place!" Darby exclaimed, tilting his head to examine it more closely, because of course it didn't look anything like it did now. Not to mention it was challenging to make out the landmarks with people streaming all over the place. "I haven't been to that one in a while."

"No one has. Lockland uses the one near The Middle, and I usually use the one near the canals," I said. "This is too close to Government Square. I hadn't thought about it before, but look." Using my other hand, I traced another path toward the government building we were trying to access. "It's all connected. This network of tunnels leads us to within twenty or so meters of this room." I tapped the room that hopefully contained the working medi-pod we needed to help Mary and the other seekers.

"Those underground walking routes were made for commuters once they left the zoom tunnels. But again," he cautioned, "there's no guarantee that the areas are passable now."

"I know," I said. "But lucky for us, we have lasers powerful enough to cut through rock. We're getting through one way or another."

Chapter 11

I paced the entire length of the room for a second time. We'd pored over the hologram map, ogling all the new sights like a bunch of little kids experiencing their first ride in a dronecraft, reiterating our plan to work our way through the old zoom tunnels to get to one of the basement entrances of the government building.

Getting that medi-pod was within our reach.

Once we had the beginnings of a plan in place, I realized Bender and Lockland should've been back from Port Station. I passed Case, who sat on a stool by the cooling unit. "I'm giving them three more minutes," I told him. "Then I'm going after them."

He nodded. "Lockland specified two hours."

"It's been more than two. Let's take Seven." I turned and headed for the main door, not willing to wait any longer. If the Bureau of Truth had found them in Port Station, things could get dangerous fast. I called over my shoulder to Darby and Daze, who were in the back with their heads together, trying to figure out where Dixon could've hidden his logs, "We're going to meet up with Lockland and Bender and see where they are."

Daze jumped up, racing toward us. "I want to go, too!" He rushed up so fast, I braced my arms in front of me so he didn't crash into my torso, toppling us both.

I shook my head as my hands settled on his shoulders. "Not this time. We're only going as a precaution. I need you to stay here with Darby and keep searching. We need Dixon's notes yesterday. If we find them, they'll likely give us vital information on the Bureau of Truth. That's the most important thing. Now that we have access to such a detailed, interactive map, we can start to put all the pieces together. It's a top priority, and you're just the guy for the job." The disappointment on his face was apparent. By his reaction, he wasn't ready for us to be apart again for a lengthy amount of time. I hadn't realized he'd been holding in his anxiety. I would be more careful next time. I bent over. "Daze, I promise this is going to be a quick run to Port Station. If something went wrong, Bender and Lockland could be in the middle of a fight, and that's not the place for you. We have to make sure they're okay. Times are…different now. We have to take extra precautions." Checking up on Bender and Lockland was new. The heightened risk we faced with the Bureau of Truth, among other things, amplified everything.

Daze reluctantly took a step back. "Okay." His voice

quavered a little, but not too much. "Darby and I will keep looking for Dixon's stuff. I'm sure we can find something. There's lots of hidey-holes around here."

"I'm sure you can, too," I said. "We have to assume Dixon was smart, not like Hutch. You have to think the way he would. I know you can do it."

He nodded as Maisie's voice came out of his pocket. "Intelligence is representative of the ability to gather and retain knowledge," she said. "The end result is to apply it to a set of skills with success."

"Maisie's right," I said, turning to leave. "Have her help you. Maybe Dixon left his notes on etch boards or some sort of software she can pick up on." I turned to Case, who had the door open, waiting. "Did you ever see Dixon using etch boards?"

He shook his head. "No. But he did speak into a recorder once in a while." My eyebrows rose, but before I could comment, Case disappeared into the hallway.

"I'm not sure if Maisie can detect recording software, but we'll give it a try." Darby stood behind Daze. "We'll be fine. Hurry back."

"We will." I left, shutting the door behind me.

Case was already cranking the lever that opened the main entrance to the barracks. If he didn't do it right, it would explode. It gave a loud thunk as the dead bolts disengaged, and he heaved it open enough for us to pass through. The sound of the crashing surf thumped against my chest as I headed toward the pilot side. It was a bummer not to have Luce here, but right now I was grateful for Seven's speed.

Case didn't argue when I took my place at the helm, and once we were up and out, heading toward Port Station, I glanced his way. "I'm debating whether we should use the tech phone or not. What you think?" I asked.

By his expression, he was surprised I'd asked his opinion. "If it was me, I wouldn't. They have to be listening in," he said. "If we're left with no other choice, then maybe, but let's wait and see."

I nodded. "Lockland said something about the outbuildings near the gates as their location for the meet. Do you think it's the same entrance we used last time we went in on foot to get Luce?"

"Could be," Case said. "I found out about that way in from my source, and there's a possibility we use the same guy. He's a greedy bastard with no scruples and very little human dignity."

"Okay," I said. "Let's head there. I'll park a kilometer out and we'll walk in." There was silence between us for a few minutes, but I felt like I had to say something about what we'd uncovered about his past. For the first time since I'd met the outskirt, there might actually be an end to feeling like he was hiding something. "You know, Case, how I see it, there's no shame in staying with Dixon as long as you did, even if the terms weren't exactly in your favor. He provided you with resources, freed you from a bad situation, and made sure you were trained and fed. It could've been worse."

"I'm not ashamed," Case replied in a monotone.

"Then why are you acting like you are?" I asked. "Your whole demeanor screams stoic with a side of pissed off. If you're okay with how things went, why not say so? It doesn't matter to us. In uncovering what we did, we were just searching for the truth." *And we're almost there, so don't ruin it.*

"Ashamed and okay are two separate things," he muttered, angling his head toward the passenger window. I waited for him to respond, which he finally did after a few moments. "I knew who Dixon was and what he was looking for when he saved me. I filled that role because I felt like it."

"A man like Dixon wields power in our world," I said. "He came in, killed everyone, freed you, provided for you, but that kind of aid usually comes with expectations of repayment. And most of the time, it's more than the person can afford to pay. I've encountered people like Dixon my entire life. They're a lot like Tandor and Hutch, but with a moral compass slightly skewed in a more positive direction. People like Dixon might be *trying* to do good, but they can't fully switch the dial. The need for power is too strong—greed, coin—it all plays a part. I'm glad life with him wasn't too hard on you."

"I didn't say it wasn't hard," Case countered with an edge.

Dixon had likely kept Case in the dark about his plans, probably threatening to leave him in the wasteland to fend for himself if he didn't cooperate. A perfect mixture of loyalty and cruelty designed to control a boy who'd had a tumultuous upbringing, never knowing where the next roof or meal might be. It had worked. For a while.

"You killed him, didn't you?" I asked, slowing our cruising speed as we approached the outer boundary of Port Station.

"Yes."

"Good."

Finally, everything Case had told me up until this point seemed to be in the right order. Maybe if he'd told us from the get-go that he'd killed Dixon, without first proving we could trust him, we might've been too suspicious to allow him into the group. In an odd way, the story needed to come out like it had, with him painting the man as his savior at first.

"I just want to remind you that we're not like Dixon," I said. "Remember that. You're free to come and go as you please. Our group isn't ruled by the fist. We run as a democracy, something our ancient ancestors lost track of somewhere along the way." Thirty years before the meteor strike, the government was run by a large oligarchy made up of rich companies and elite individuals with special interests, not a democracy like it had for hundreds of years prior. "We don't keep information from each other that can keep us alive. We share it because we *want* to."

Case said nothing, but I didn't expect him to.

As we flew closer to Port Station, I recognized the area where Case had set us down when we were here last. Remembering directions and specific locations was important for a salvager. Four trees in a group to the right, one boulder to the left, proximity to a large ditch three meters south.

I slowed to a stop and eased Seven down on her landing pads.

Shutting the props off, I leaned forward to glance out the windshield. It was the middle of the day. I'd never approached Port Station in the daytime, which was odd.

We got out, and I flipped my visor down. "Let's go." We began to jog toward the area that would lead us near Daze's old residence. We ran in silence, until we heard shouting. "That was Bender," I said as we picked up the pace, racing through a sparse forest of dead trees, our weapons out.

When a group of broken outbuildings came into view, I caught a glimpse of Bender and then Lockland.

With relief, I saw they were both fine. They had their weapons trained on a man kneeling in front of them.

Case and I slowed. Lockland looked up, meeting my eyes across the expanse. "What are you doing here?" he called.

"It's been over two hours." As we paced closer, I spotted another body crumpled on the ground to the right, blood pooling from a number of wounds. Lockland had used his Blaster. "Looks like we missed all the action." Case and I stopped in front of them.

"The asshole tried to turn us in." Bender gestured to the dead guy.

"Turn you in to who?" I asked.

"That's not important," Lockland said. "Before he could do so, this Bureau of Truth agent arrived on the scene."

I moved around the man to stand next to Lockland so I could see his face. "This guy is from the bureau? Are you sure?"

"Not one hundred percent," Lockland said. "He won't say either way, but that's my guess."

"And he just showed up here?" I glanced around, not spotting anything out of the ordinary. We were still a good thirty meters from the opening in the wall that ran around Port Station.

"Once he got here, they both tried to play it off like it was part of the plan," Bender said. "The guy who died"—he jammed his thumb in the body's direction—"said he had a partner he wanted to bring in, but we could see he was scared. Then he drew his weapon."

"He might've been trying to finesse a side deal," I said. The man on his knees was helmetless, his dark curly hair plastered to his face. He had an angry look in his eyes and looked to be intelligent. He was definitely sizing me up. I glanced at Lockland, who nodded, giving me the okay. Casually, with my Gem out, I took a few steps to place myself directly in front of him, making sure his eyes were riveted on me. Quicker than he could anticipate, I kicked him in the chest. He arched over, landing on his back. I followed, bringing a knee down, jamming it straight into his abdomen right below the breastbone. His breath whooshed out as he gasped for air. I let up a tiny bit so he could breathe. Then I grinned. "Are you with the Bureau of Truth?"

He struggled to catch his breath, giving me the look I'd expected. Like I was the novice and he was the superior.

"We already asked him that," Bender growled.

"Yeah, I figured," I said. "But this is how I work. I like it when they underestimate me." My gaze lingered on the man, who was now breathing somewhat evenly, my knee still on his chest. "I didn't think you'd answer that, but you don't have to. I'm assuming by what my friends told me that you're here alone. You were probably sent to snoop around and keep your eye on things and report back." I glanced up at Lockland. "Is he wearing an amplifier? Does he have a tech phone?"

"Neither," Lockland said.

I grinned again, this time with a full-out chuckle.

"What's so funny?" Bender asked.

"You two are forgetting something," I said.

"What's that?" Bender asked, his biceps jumping as he crossed his arms.

"We have Babble."

Chapter 12

"Who's there?" The voice resonated with panic. "I have a wicked laser gun, and I'm not afraid to use it. If you come in, I'll shoot, and it will hurt bad."

"Ned?" I called through the door, tossing Case a confused look. After leaving Bender and Lockland, who were taking the prisoner back to the barracks, we'd been tasked with sneaking into the city to get the Babble. "What are you doing here?" I heard soft moans a second later. "Is Mary in there with you?"

The door whipped open a second later, and a relieved Ned collapsed in the jamb. "I had no choice." He urged us into the room, shutting the door behind us. It was dark inside, save for his shoulder light, so I clicked mine on, making my way over to Mary. "I didn't know where else to go," he continued. "There are UACs all over outside, and at one point I heard voices. I didn't want them to find us."

We'd suspected the same thing. That was why we

were two buildings away, instead of at the Emporium, where the Babble was stored. Finding Ned and Mary was a total surprise.

"I'm glad you're safe," I said as I knelt beside the woman whom I hoped to meet as her true self one day. She was fairly lucid, lying on top of a scummy-looking blanket. "Have you given her more Plush recently?" I hated that we were giving the drug to her.

Ned knelt beside me. "I gave her some before we left. I had to. She was making all kinds of noise. I couldn't get her through the tube without it."

I sat back on my haunches, facing him. "How did you know about the pneumatic tube?" A transit system had been constructed to pass through the building between the Emporium and this one. According to data I'd found a time long ago, Bliss Corp owned both buildings, but not the one in between, so they'd had to purchase the rights to a portion of the building to make it happen. It'd probably cost an obscene amount of money to build. The tube had been touted as "a passageway through which to bring in supplies," but the fine print had said it was for transporting elite clients to and from the Pleasure Emporium out of the public eye.

It went without saying that the rich and famous hadn't wanted their movements known when visiting the Pleasure Emporium, and I was sure they'd paid a lofty price for it.

The tube itself had housed a travel car that people would've been seated in as they'd been shot at high speeds through the building. In order to access the transit system now, depending on which direction you were coming from, you had to climb up or down a two-story maintenance shaft to enter. If you came from the Emporium side, you had to jump on top of the travel car, climb through an opening someone had hacked in the roof of the vehicle, and head out of the blown-out rear and crawl through the tube. From this side, we'd access the tube first, crawl through the wrecked car, and out the top.

The entire system had remained intact only because it'd been extremely well-built out of super-thick steel and was located right above the water line. I'd used it only a couple times, because it was a pain to crawl through the tube for that long, and once I'd salvaged a few times around the area, there had been no need to revisit. Until now.

"I didn't know about it until Darby told me a few days ago," Ned said. "I think someone in your group said something about it before you guys left town. They instructed me to use it in case of emergency." That made sense. Bender and Lockland both knew about it.

"Well," I said, "I'm super impressed you got Mary up and down those skinny ladders. In fact, it kind of boggles the mind you were able to do it." I stood, glancing around the small space, a former interior office of some kind. It was the first room after exiting up and out of the tunnel. Not a super-great hideout if whoever was after them knew about the tube.

"Yeah," Ned said, absentmindedly flicking his hair. "I had to use some rope, but we made it." He gaped at me like he was seeing me for the first time. "But what are you doing here? How did you know we would be here?"

"We didn't. We just happened upon you. We came to get Babble to interrogate the guy we captured and figured the Bureau of Truth was monitoring things, so we came this way."

"Bureau of what?" Ned asked, his brows furrowing.

"Never mind. The good news is, once we have the Babble, things should be figured out within a day or two. Do you think you're okay to stay here with Mary until then?" It wasn't ideal. I spotted a small duffel on the ground. "Do you have enough food and water?"

"Yeah, I have enough for a couple days. But I don't have any Plush left. I used it all."

I nodded. "Okay." I glanced down at Mary, who seemed to be fairly peaceful for the moment. "Then we'll just have to work faster."

Case grunted, "How exactly do you propose we do that? We've been going at breakneck speed."

I shrugged as I moved past him. "We use our legs and make them work harder." At the door, I turned, addressing Ned. "Do you really have a wicked laser gun?"

"No," he answered as he lifted his waistband. "I just have this."

A half-tase. "That will do. But the element of surprise is important. If anyone else comes here, don't announce yourself and don't panic. Open the door and hit them with it, keeping your finger on the trigger as long as you can. But I don't think that'll be necessary. If these guys knew about the tube, they'd already be here. When we leave, lodge something in front of the door. If we're not back within two days, you're going to have to move Mary again."

Ned looked a little confused, but rallied. "Okay. I understand."

"If you have to go, get her out of the canals. Head someplace familiar. How about Dill's?" We'd been there together, and I could find it again.

He nodded. "I'll do that."

With one hand on the knob, I said, "I promise we're going to get Mary to that medi-pod."

Ned's eyes were solemn as he responded, "I believe you."

I shut the door.

Case stood by the maintenance entrance. "You were right," he said with no further clarification as he mounted the ladder and began to climb down the two stories needed to get to the tube.

"And you're surprised about that?" I asked as I followed. I didn't even have to ask him what he was talking about. Of course I was right.

"I'm talking about coming this route, instead of going directly to the Emporium," Case said with a chuckle.

"Again, and you're surprised?" After a few moments, I said, "I've been thinking about something. It's a little strange that the UACs chose now to come after Dixon's craft, since you've been buzzing around the city for a couple of months now. They had to have known you were here before. It's a possibility they left you alone because they thought you were with Tandor, but now that they know you're not, they're pursuing you. I think it's all tied together. Tandor and his group definitely had something to do with the Bureau of Truth."

Case reached the bottom of the ladder before responding, jumping down the last few rungs, his footsteps echoing up the shaft. I still had my shoulder light on, soft blue effusing the small space around us. "I've been running over those same things in my mind." Case made room for me to land, ducking down to begin our crawl through the tube. "It feels like it's all connected somehow. But I have no idea how the Bureau of Truth could've brokered a deal with Tandor. The only thing that possibly connects those two are the militia factions down South."

"Exactly," I said. "And if all the militias are somehow working together, with the Bureau of Truth at the head, it means that Tandor's trip up here might've been a trial run. He could've been a sacrifice sent to the big city to see who would act up in the face of an overthrow. If that was their plan, we played right into it. No one acted up more than we did—in fact, we reacted so hard, we ended up killing Tandor and most of his men."

"Yeah," he said. "It's going to take some time to unravel. If the Bureau of Truth is a pseudo-government group working with the militias to infiltrate and tear down the current structure, it's one hell of a network."

I didn't want to think about all those implications just yet. If the scope was that big, the task seemed insurmountable.

One thing at a time.

We finally made it to the other end of the tube, coming up on the old pneumatic car that had privately zoomed rich clients looking for a good time to the Pleasure Emporium. We picked our way through the wreckage of the transport, which held six seats, and made our way out the top, where someone long before we'd been here had made a hole in the roof.

The next maintenance shaft was directly above us, but the first rung was farther off the ground than I remembered. Either Case or I would need a boost. "How do you want to work this?" I asked.

He answered by intertwining his fingers and bending over. I placed my boot in his hand, springing off the ground as he shot me upward. My gloved hands encompassed the cold steel. I hoisted myself up easily, hooking my knees around the bottom rung, bending my torso back down, and extending an arm.

Case grabbed on, and I hauled him up, crunching my waist, one hand reaching up for the rung above me for leverage. It took every ounce of strength I had. "How much do you weigh anyway?" I groaned. It felt like a hundred and fifty kilos.

"I have no idea," he grunted, reaching out for the bottom rung as I scooted to the side. Once he had both hands on the steel, I pulled my legs out and continued up the ladder.

It felt longer going up than it had coming down. Once we reached the top, I was breathing hard. We still had several more stories to go to reach the lab, but thankfully, we were going to use a staircase instead of a ladder.

"There are four stairwells to choose from," I said, bracing my hands on my thighs for a second to catch my breath. The Emporium occupied the upper floors, but the entire building had been Bliss Corp offices. When we arrived back in town a few days ago, I'd done some scouting—pretty much for emergencies just like this one. "Two within twenty meters of center. Darby's lab is located on the south end of the building on the floor we occupy. I say we start up the south stairwell and hope it's clear." During my scouting process, I hadn't run all four stairways top to bottom. That would've taken too much time. "Unless you have a better plan?"

"Sounds good to me," Case said.

We headed that direction.

The damage on this floor was extensive, the place in shambles. If the infrastructure hadn't been constructed so well, with no expense spared and steel beams and girders exceeding the load specifications, this building would've been done for long ago.

We had no idea if bureau agents might be inside the building, or only staking out the airspace above, so we had to move cautiously. We traversed four stories, sidestepping and mucking through a ton of garbage. Rounding the fourth-story landing, we encountered a pile of trash taller than we were.

I stuck my head into the middle of the stairway and glanced up. "It's completely impassable from here on." Large chunks of wall and ceiling tiles had caved in, blocking the way for several stories above us.

"Let's try to see if this floor is passable," Case said as he eased the door open. It was barely set on its hinges and made a loud groaning noise.

We both paused, listening.

"I'm just guessing here, because it's hard to keep track of where we are," I murmured, "but I think the Pleasure Emporium is at least four to six stories above where we're standing now." He nodded as we slipped into the hallway.

Halfway down, Case stopped and set his head toward a small window cut into a door. All the signage had long eroded, but it looked like the entrance to a stairwell to me.

He opened it, and we went through.

Chapter 13

"I think this is it," I whispered. We'd just rounded the fifth landing in the new stairwell, which had contained much less trash and had been easier to traverse. Case laid his ear against the door. When he deemed it clear, he eased it open no more than a couple centimeters, adjusting the position of his head so he would detect anything in the hallway.

A second later, his arm shot up, catching my attention.

He'd heard something.

I crept closer. He murmured, "Voices. At least two."

"Damn." That's not what I wanted to hear. "It's going to be hard to sneak by people who are lying in wait for us," I said, my voice low. We had no choice. We had to get to the Babble. "Maybe we can sneak into the lab and retrieve the vials, then escape without them detecting us."

Case slowly shook his head. "Highly unlikely. We

have to find out where they're located first. But if I open the door any wider, it's going to make noise."

My Gem was out and ready. I drew my taser. "We have to do this. Lockland and Bender are waiting for us back at the barracks. The information that guy will give us is priceless."

Case nodded. "I'll open it. You go through first. I'll follow."

"Any time you're ready," I told him, bending my arms, propping my elbows against my rib cage for maximum support. Case opened it and, for once, a door I was using didn't make a sound.

I entered the hallway at a crouch, both arms extended in front of me. It took me only a few moments to realize we were on the wrong floor, likely one below the Emporium. That meant whoever was here staking us out expected us to arrive from above, not from a stairwell on this floor.

Bonus.

Case came into the hallway behind me, the door closing with a soft whoosh. The two male voices were coming from a room on the right. I moved to the other side of the hallway and made my way closer. Someone had shoved all the trash against one wall, which made it much easier to navigate.

"This is bullshit," a guy said, his voice low and raspy. "There's no way they're coming back here."

"A job's a job. What are you going to do?" another guy answered, his voice higher and rushed.

"I can't believe these people think they can go up against Bender's crew. Don't they know anything about this city?"

So, we were "Bender's crew" to the public? Interesting.

"If I had to guess, I'd say they're government," the guy with the higher voice said.

"Nah," the other one replied. "If they were government, they never would've hired us."

"What you mean? We can do surveillance just as good as anyone else."

I'd have to vote a hard *no* on that. Case and I were already within three meters of their location, and they had no idea we were here. The good thing was, we were dealing with hired help, not the bureau. And I agreed with the first guy. Why would a group like the Bureau of Truth hire amateurs?

"No, we can't," the raspy guy challenged, echoing my thoughts exactly. "We've never even seen this kind of tech before. All we've ever done was use a few amplifiers."

"The monitors do the work for us," the whiny guy said. "If we see something, all we have to do is call them on this."

I couldn't see what *this* was, but I assumed it was a tech phone, and if he was citing monitors, that meant they had a live video feed set up.

"I think it's pretty awesome," the whiner wheezed.

"You know what's not going to be awesome?"

"What?"

"When Bender finds out. I live in The Middle," the raspy one said. "If he discovers it was me who ratted him out, I'm dead."

Good. If they feared Bender more than whoever had employed them, then the chances of flipping their loyalty with a few coins ran high.

"Yeah," the first guy agreed. "I've never seen him up close, but there are plenty of stories in the skells about him."

They were confirming that Bender was a legend, which was not a shocker. I grinned, thinking Bender was going to enjoy hearing what these guys had to say.

I was about to make a move to surprise them, threaten them into changing their loyalty, and quickly follow it up with a promise of coin if they cooperated, when Case grabbed my forearm.

He held me there for a second while the two men continued to talk.

"Bender would kill us, it's true," the raspy guy said. "But the other two would make it hurt."

My eyebrows rose.

"The girl, Holly, nobody messes with her. I heard she took that guy out by the cliffs by lasering holes through both his legs before she shot him in the face. The other guy, Lockland, he's like that, too, but he carries a Blaster. He'll pump multiple rounds into you before he finishes the job."

Well, well, well.

Bender was a legend, but apparently Lockland and I were also notorious.

No part of me enjoyed watching someone suffer in death, but threatening to make them hurt to gain needed information was different. I didn't mind being notorious. It got the job done. If these guys believed I was capable of such things, it worked in my favor.

"Yeah," the whiny guy said. "I heard the girl never smiles. Like, ever."

Hey. I smiled. Sometimes.

"Some people say she's a LiveBot created by Bender as a weapon. That guy has a talent for fixing things, so I can believe it," the raspy guy said. "Who knows what he builds in that shop? He could have a bunch of them ready to go."

I wasn't even close to being a LiveBot.

But I was excellent at role-play.

I pivoted into the room, a weapon aimed in each man's direction. Their faces dropped comically as fear became the common denominator.

"Put your hands up," I ordered in my best unemotional, Maisie-like tone, careful to keep any expression off my face. "State your mission, or I shoot and you die." For good measure, I added, "But I'll make it hurt first."

The guys crashed into each other trying to hoist their arms. One was taller than the other by a good half meter. He spoke first. "We were hired to keep watch on the floor above." He flicked his index finger at the ceiling. He was the one with the whiny voice. "But only to watch," he said hastily. "We don't have any weapons on us. I swear!"

"Yeah," the shorter, raspy guy said. "Don't shoot. We mean no harm. We just wanted the coin."

"Who hired you?" I asked, still channeling a computer-modulated voice, my expression fixed, my body unmoving.

The taller guy shrugged. "We don't know. They found him"—he jabbed his thumb toward the shorter guy—"at Lodenbat's skell. Do you know where it is?" I nodded once, choosing not to speak, waiting for him to fill in the gaps, which he did in a rush. "They offered us a lot of coin, too much to refuse, but that's it. They brought us here, gave us a phone, and told us what to do. But they're not due back until tomorrow."

"Hand your communication devices to my assistant." I jutted my chin out, cocking my head to the right in a stiff movement to indicate Case, who had come in behind me.

Both of the men gasped.

It seemed the LiveBot act was easy to fall for when you'd never seen a robot before and your preconceived notions precluded common sense. They each scrabbled over the table, trying to grasp the phone, knocking things off as they went.

"Um, we only have the one," the raspy guy said, winning the battle, dropping the tech phone into Case's open palm.

"What security measures have they implemented above?" I asked.

The taller guy rubbed the back of his neck. "They didn't tell us any of that."

I flicked my wrists up and down twice, indicating that they should both put their hands back up. They raised them fast.

"My helper is going to stay here with you while I retrieve something Bender requires from upstairs. Then the two of you are going to disappear and tell no one you were here." They both nodded frantically. "And if you break our confidence, I will hunt you down and go after your—"

"We know, our families," the whiny guy stammered. "We won't betray you. I swear. We didn't even want to be here in the first place."

"When Bender finds out, he will not be happy." I made sure my eyes bored into the shorter guy, who had indicated he lived in The Middle.

"Does he have to know?" he replied, his tone nearly mirroring his pal's whine for a moment. "I mean, we're fully cooperating. We'll even give back the coin! We want no trouble."

I shook my head, making the movements quick and jerky. "Keep the coin." Both of their faces reflected surprise. "The men who gave it to you will have no use for it when we're done with them." Then, with a dramatic flair, I holstered both of my weapons at the same time and turned, keeping my body stiff as I marched out of the room.

It didn't matter if they actually believed in the end that I was a LiveBot. The ruse had worked for the moment and made our task here easier than it probably would've been otherwise. I was usually a good judge of character—well, until Case had come along—but by the look of fear on their faces, we could trust them. At least for the next few days, which was all we needed.

Once we defeated the bureau, none of this would matter.

Instead of going up the middle staircase, I jogged to the end of the hallway, right under where the lab was supposed to be upstairs. I pushed the door open, checking to see if the stairwell here was passable. It didn't look too bad. I moved inside, tugging some big chunks of wall out of the way.

I made it up to the next level, placing my ear against the door.

No sounds that I could detect.

It would be silly not to think the bureau had planted traps. After all, getting rid of us was probably their first choice. But coming in the back way would definitely reduce the chances of me stumbling onto something nasty. The roof and the main entrance would be their focus.

I nudged the door open a centimeter at a time. When it was open as wide as an eyeball, I did an infrared scan with my visor down. Then I clicked my visor up and grabbed my chromes out of my vest. They were an old pair, the x-ray setting damaged, but they were the best I had as a replacement for the pair that had been disintegrated by the radium ball.

Flicking through the dial, I checked the gammas and ultraviolet. If there were bombs in plain sight, they should give me an indication.

Everything appeared clear.

Easing the door wider, I stepped out. I had no idea where the video feeds were located, or if they covered the hallway this far down, but I knew Case was monitoring the situation from below, which, oddly, made me feel better.

I couldn't wait to see his face when this was all over. I hadn't consulted him about the LiveBot plan, as it had been a gut reaction. Calling him my assistant had been a stroke of genius, but I was fairly certain he wouldn't think so, which made it that much sweeter.

That thought hadn't been out of my head for two seconds before a muffled sound came from behind me.

Shit.

"We knew you'd come bac—"

I didn't give the guy a chance to finish. Men. They were always so chatty. Twisting my hips, I brought my boot up, hacking it into the side of his neck. He was short, so that helped. He hit the wall and bounced off, his weapon clattering to the floor.

I'd holstered my taser, leaving a hand free so I could grab his forearm. Using the forward motion, I twisted him in a circle and launched him down the hallway. He landed on his back, skidding toward the entrance of the Emporium, before he crashed headfirst into a wall and came to a stop.

Both hands on my Gem, arms stretched in front of me, I jogged forward. He came off the ground, bracing himself on one arm. I kicked it out from under him, snapping the bone. He collapsed back on the floor, moaning.

"Who are you and what do you want with us?" I didn't expect him to answer. I was just asking as a formality, so when he did it surprised me.

"I'm from an elite group that has more firepower than you," he ground out. "You're not going to win this."

"What exactly am I trying to win?" If I could get this guy to talk, it would be a win.

"Control," he said with a smirk.

This guy was acting too smug. Something was up. He should've been fearful, or at the very least feral. He'd lost his weapon, his arm was broken, and I had him in a compromising position. Yet he brimmed with confidence and something else I couldn't pinpoint.

What was I missing? My gaze darted around the hallway.

Then I saw it.

He tracked my gaze, his face dropping. He turned suddenly, reaching toward the trip wire that would likely trigger a bomb that would blow us all up.

"Not today, elite guy," I said.

I fired my Gem.

It wasn't pretty.

Chapter 14

"Just stay on course," I grumbled. "Your amusement is freaking me out. You don't process emotions, remember?"

"Well…" Case chuckled. "It's not often I get to witness someone pretend to be a LiveBot and actually succeed. Then, when you flung that guy down the hallway straight into the live-feed monitor and blew a hole through his neck, I think one of the guys actually wet himself."

"I didn't have a choice," I groused. "He would've blown us all up if he'd had his way. I inspected the bomb after, and it was massive. It would've taken out both floors. It's going to take both Bender and Lockland to disarm that place. I'm just glad the lab was clear." I patted my vest where I'd stashed the vials of Babble.

"You don't have to worry about those guys telling anyone," Case affirmed. "They'll be scurrying home and staying there."

I arched an eyebrow at him. "I wasn't worried." After I'd come back, the two of them had fallen all over themselves to swear their allegiance to "Bender's crew." Even though I hadn't put much effort into the LiveBot performance in the end, I'd seen the looks on their faces once we released them. They still weren't quite certain whether I was one or not.

The rumors were going to be rampant, which I didn't mind. Uncertainty gave me an advantage.

Running a gloved hand over my face, I leaned back against the headrest while Case piloted the craft. We'd be at the barracks in a few minutes. We'd successfully hidden Seven out of sight of the Bureau of Truth and made it out of the city without a tail. Most likely, they hadn't anticipated we'd come back, even though they'd been monitoring the building.

"What I don't understand," I started, "is why the guy in the hallway was so willing to sacrifice his life. Not only willing—he seemed eager to do it. It doesn't add up. There isn't a cause great enough to blow yourself up. There hasn't been a martyr to any cause in over sixty years, at least that I know about. It's every man, woman, and child for themselves." I tilted my reclined head toward Case. "Now would be a really good time for you to remember anything Dixon might've said, even in passing, about the bureau."

Case gave an almost imperceptible sigh. "We can't keep doing this. I told you everything—"

"I'm not talking about what you *think* is valuable information. I'm talking about day-to-day stuff. Habits

Dixon might've had that he picked up while he was working for the secret pseudo-government agency, or quirky things he would say, or how he swore under his breath—literally anything that would help us figure out what's going on. If that guy back there was willing to blow himself up, there has to be some kind of loyalty pledge or something. If there's not, it doesn't make any sense."

"If members of that group were forced to take a pledge that they would die for their cause, then that's exactly why Dixon got the hell out," Case said, his teeth on edge. It was the first negative thing I'd heard him say about Dixon. "There was nothing further from a martyr than Dixon. The man was all about protecting himself and hoarding resources." I watched as Case's knuckles whitened as he tightened his hands on Seven's levers. "I can't think of anything right now that he used to do regularly, but I'll let you know."

"Thank you," I said, meaning it. Having a completely normal interaction with Case about his past wasn't usual. After a moment, I added, "And I'm sorry." I held up my hand. "Before you get bent out of shape, it's not the pity kind of sorry. It's a legitimate I'm-sorry-your-life-was-so-shitty sorry. I got out at nine. You didn't get out until six months ago. The bottom line is that it sucks, and I'm sorry. If it's any consolation, nobody else is going to mess with you anymore. Especially not when you're going to be seen around town as part of 'Bender's crew.'" I laid my hand back in my lap, stretching my shoulders and lower back. "And of course, once those two guys we just let loose start the gossip going, you'll be known as the guy in the company of the only working LiveBot in the history of the world—except for Trina down South." Images of that battered LiveBot, with her lifelike skin hanging off her face in ribbons, popped very unwelcomely into my mind. "You're totally covered."

Case chuckled. The clarity and resonance of the sound were strange enough to make me turn. The man actually sounded *happy*. And not just the mimicking happy either. I wasn't familiar with this relaxed Case. "The LiveBot impersonation will serve you well."

"I hope so," I said. He turned his gaze on me, where it lingered for a few moments. It was hard not to feel exposed. "What?"

"I've never met anyone who can think on their feet as fast as you can." His voice was low. "It's an incredible thing to witness."

I had no idea what to say.

The compliment was completely unexpected. I opted for a conversational response. "If you can't think fast, your chances of getting killed rise considerably. It's a necessary adaptation for survival. We all do it."

He shook his head. "No. I mean, yes, we do. But your talent for it supersedes anyone I've ever seen before. You seem to anticipate things at a greater rate. In order to do that, you have to be evaluating your surroundings continuously."

"You're forgetting the fact that you successfully surprised me at Daze's residence. You tossed me out a second-story window, and you and the kid both managed to play me a number of times." I was still pissed at myself about that. "I'm not infallible, nor am I superhuman. I try not to get played, because I want to survive, but it's nothing more than that."

"You got played for a reason."

I gaped at him. I couldn't help it. "What exactly does that mean?"

"You trust people you care about, even if you don't want to," he answered with no sign of smugness.

I was saved from replying as he took us out over the sea, angling us into the barracks parking space seamlessly. Once we landed, I thought about arguing my point, but decided to drop it. And maybe, possibly, there might be a kernel of truth to what he'd said.

By the time I came around the passenger side, Case was already working on the main door. He'd given both Bender and Lockland the code to unlock it, and since nothing had blown, I assumed they'd been successful, unless they'd gone through the hatch, which was a possibility. Bender had likely dropped off Lockland and the bureau guy and gone to park the craft elsewhere, walking back.

As we pushed into the main room, Daze jumped up. "You're back!"

I walked in, glancing around the empty space.

The tech table was on, the hologram map of the city up, letting me know what Darby and Daze had been up to.

Darby read my face right, stopping in front of me. "What's wrong?"

"Where are Lockland and Bender?" I asked, my tone pointed. "They're supposed to be here."

"They haven't come back yet," Darby said.

Behind me, Case had already exited the room, likely to go back out to start up Seven. "Come on," I told Daze and Darby. They wasted no time following. "Lockland and Bender must have encountered some trouble," I explained as we paced quickly down the hallway. "We left them with a guy they'd caught, someone we think is from the bureau. They were supposed to come directly back here. Case and I went to get the Babble from the Emporium so we could interrogate him." I swore. "We're not using our tech phones, so we didn't check in. I just assumed they wouldn't have any issues." They shouldn't have. The guy had been on his knees.

Once outside, I hoisted the passenger door. Case was already in the pilot seat, Seven's props going. Darby and Daze climbed into the backseat. Darby commented, "Our phones didn't make any noise."

"It was doubtful they would have," I said. "The walls in the barracks must be three meters thick. Maisie can't even get her neutrinos through them very well."

Maisie, still in Daze's pocket and recognizing her name, said, "Holly, you are correct. Although my NEUdar technology can pass through concrete and soil, its accuracy is compromised at that density."

"Well, it's not compromised anymore," I said. "It's time to work. I need you to pinpoint the location of Lockland's craft." Maisie could tell the difference between each of us and each of our crafts.

Daze pulled her out of his pocket, holding her between the seats in his open palm as Case propelled us up and over the barracks.

Maisie's lights blinked across the top of her shiny polymer egg-shaped body. After a moment, she said, "I detect three human signatures, one Lockland, one Bender, and one unknown male. Lockland's craft is disabled. Head southwest twenty-three-point-seven kilometers and you will find them." That was only a kilometer or two outside of Port Station.

I blew out a long sigh of relief. They were alive and close by. "Wait, what do you mean by 'disabled'?"

She replied, "The craft has sustained critical damage that has rendered it inoperable."

"You mean they crashed?" I asked, shocked.

"Yes, they crashed," she said.

Before I could ask the question on everyone's mind, Darby blurted, "Is everyone okay?" Then he clarified with, "Please relay detailed vitals on the three humans detected."

"Specific vitals at this distance are not accessible. Chest respirations are detected. Heart rates are increased."

Thank goodness for chest respirations and heart rates.

"The guy they took must've gotten at the controls

or something," I muttered, shaking my head. There was no other explanation. Lockland was an excellent pilot.

"Or he could be in possession of some technology that could interfere with the operating system of the craft," Darby contemplated. "That kind of technology exists. If he really is from the bureau, we can't accurately predict what they have access to."

I shifted in my seat. "Lockland and Bender would've patted him down first and checked him thoroughly. They're not amateurs."

"This kind of thing could be as tiny as a pebble," Darby said.

We'd know soon enough. Up ahead, Lockland's craft came into view. From the looks of it, she'd gone straight down, nose first, which was hard to do when you had four props below you maintaining stability. That meant the front two props had failed.

It was clear something had gone horribly wrong.

Case landed a few meters away as I began to panic. No one was near the craft. "Maisie, where are they?" I asked as I lofted my door and hopped out.

Maisie answered, "Bender, Lockland, and the unknown male are a half kilometer straight west."

I took off running, spotting Bender first. He was upright, his back propped against a tree. The other two were on the ground. By the looks of it, Bender had dragged them to this location. I rushed up, breathing heavily, sliding to a stop. "What happened? What's going on?" I landed on my knees next to Lockland, who was prone, his face tilted to the side, blood coating the side of his head. Both he and the bureau guy were out cold.

I ripped off a glove and settled my fingers against his neck. His heart rate was steady, but it seemed to slow as I counted the beats.

"He…he…" Bender struggled to speak, bracing his chest with one arm.

Behind me, Case, Darby, and Daze caught up.

Before Bender could continue, Maisie said, "Vitals on Bender. Noncritical. Four cracked ribs, small puncture to esophageal lining, major damage to right quadriceps. Recommend seeking medical aid. Vitals on Lockland. Critical. Internal bleeding, damaged spleen, shattered sternum, cracked left femur, massive concussion, significant blood loss. Medical aid necessary. Injuries are life-threatening. Vitals on unknown male—"

"Stop," I commanded. I didn't give a shit about the other guy. I moaned as I turned Lockland over. He was coated in blood. "This can't be happening."

Darby knelt next to me. "We can fix this."

His voice was so certain, I shot him a look, my brain working overtime. "The medi-pod at the barracks?"

"No," he answered. "I checked it out. It's only for minor injuries. But the medi-pod we found earlier at the abandoned building has more than enough power to heal him." He lifted one of Lockland's eyelids. Lockland didn't even twitch.

"We only have one craft," I said.

"You and I take Bender and Lockland," Darby said. "I know you can get there quick, Holly. You're the best pilot around. We can save him if we go now. We'll have to leave Case and Daze here, though, but they'll be fine. They can watch over the bureau guy until we get back."

"It's a risk. We don't know for certain if that medipod works. We didn't start it up," I said, a plea in my voice. "If we take him back to the barracks, maybe the one there can mend him partway, so he's not in danger of dying, and then we can take him to the other medipod."

"No, he's too critical. He only has one chance," Darby answered firmly. "We're wasting time. We need to go now." Darby stood.

"Leave me…the fuck here," Bender wheezed. "Take him…now."

I stood, turning in a circle, feeling bewildered. "We're not leaving you, so shut the hell up and let me think."

We weren't leaving anyone, if I could help it.

I glanced around. Case was gone.

Props sounded a second later. As he landed Seven next to us, I raced to the pilot side. As it opened, I said, "Bender's craft is by the barracks. We can fly back there, get it, and come back—"

Case got out and grabbed me by the shoulders, shaking me slightly. "There's no time. Bender and Lockland need help. We get them into this craft now. You go with Darby. Daze and I will handle things here. Come and get us when you can."

I nodded, mumbling, "Okay." He was right. There was no other way.

Rushing back to Lockland's side, I knew I had to get him to the medi-pod in time. I didn't do loss well.

Not even a little bit.

Chapter 15

Getting Lockland into the craft without exacerbating his injuries had been a huge feat. Maisie had confirmed that everything was stable once he was settled. He was currently propped across Darby's lap in the back. Bender sat next to me, holding his chest, trying to relay the story of what had happened to them as I flew at top speed.

"We checked him. I swear, we checked him," Bender said through gritted teeth. Trying to talk with four cracked ribs and a tear in your breathing tube wasn't ideal, but I needed details. "He had e-cuffs on and everything. Then, out of the blue, the craft starts powering off and on. Then the front two props stopped altogether, and we took a dive. There was no way to stop it. It happened so fast. The controls were powerless. The whole time it was going down, the guy was laughing. It was an evil sound, like he was enjoying himself."

"The same thing happened with the guy I ran into at the Emporium," I said. "He seemed eager to take himself out. It's clear these guys are willing to sacrifice themselves—and for what? It doesn't make any sense." Our speed was maxed out at about three hundred kilometers an hour. The hydro-boost hadn't been replaced since Case and I used it to outrun the UAC. But even without it, we'd be there soon.

I'd bypassed the city completely. We didn't need any more hassles.

If the bureau didn't already know they were missing two guys, they would soon, and I was positive there would be a full-scale counterattack. Setting foot inside the city limits, especially in Seven, would be asking for a war now.

"I'm pretty sure that asshole electrocuted himself when we crashed. His e-cuffs came off," Bender growled, stifling a cough. "But I didn't see any other injuries. He was in the back."

"Case will figure it out," I said. "I left Maisie with them. She'll know what's wrong with him." We had no idea how long it would take Lockland to heal once he was inside the medi-pod, but when he was safe, I'd go back to retrieve Case and Daze. It wasn't ideal, but Daze had rallied us, encouraging me to go. Still, the whole setup made me uneasy. They were too close to Port Station for my liking, with no way to escape.

"That bastard was lucky I didn't kill him with my bare hands," Bender said. "But if he dies, we lose everything in his head. I couldn't risk it."

"How come you dragged them so far?" I asked. "You weren't exactly in any shape to do that."

He shrugged, then winced. "Because I figured the crash made enough noise for someone in Port Station to notice, and I didn't want us out in the open like easy targets. I knew once you got back to the barracks and saw we weren't there, you'd come find us. But it felt like it took you fucking forever."

"I'm sorry," I said. "The process to get the Babble took some time. The bureau hired some hacks to do surveillance. They were easily sidestepped, but they had a man of their own waiting on our floor." I left out all the LiveBot stuff. I'd fill him in later.

"Make sure nothing happens to those vials," Bender said. "We almost died. I want it to count."

"It will."

In the back, Lockland moaned. Concerned, I turned, asking Darby, "Is he okay?"

"His pulse is irregular, but he's holding," Darby said. "For how long, I don't know. Hurry."

"Working on it," I said. "According to my internal directions, the building should be fifteen kilometers up and to the right. The edge of the roof should be visible shortly." Within moments, the roofline came into view. One part was caved in. The rest stood out starkly against the dead forest around it. I didn't slow.

"Whoa," Bender said. "You have to back off, or—"

At the last minute, I jammed my right hand to the side and my left straight down. The craft spun one hundred and eighty degrees as it dropped rapidly. Just as we were about to make impact, I momentarily went to full throttle to slow our descent, and we touched down. I'd managed to do it smoothly enough not to jar us too much, making a banked landing right where I'd set down before. I shut off the props and unbuckled my harness, opening my door almost simultaneously. Bender wasn't moving. Instead, he stared at me, looking puzzled. "What?" I asked.

"I didn't know you could do that."

"There are a lot of things you don't know about me." I got out and hustled around to the other side. "Just wait, you stubborn oaf." Bender was in the process of trying to extract himself on his own. "You have mangled quadriceps. How you managed to drag two grown men half a kilometer, I'll never know." I wasn't superhuman, but there was a possibility Bender was. Jamming my shoulder into his armpit, I took his weight and hoisted him out. Once he was a few meters clear, I went back to the craft, bending through the door. "Darby, you're going to have to climb out first. I need you inside starting up that machine. Lockland has to go over my shoulder, which is going to put pressure on his insides." I winced. Lockland weighed over a hundred kilos, but there was no other way. I could manage it, but it would take everything I had. "The pod has to be ready to go once we get inside."

"I can help you," Bender said gruffly behind me. "You take his shoulders, I'll take his feet."

"You're in no shape—"

"Don't talk to me about what I can and can't do."

Bender's words practically ended on a roar. "I can stand the pain. I'm taking a ride in that medi-pod after Lockland, and this shit will end. What I have is mild compared to him. He'd do the same for me. Let's go." I gave him a long look and finally nodded. Darby scrambled out as Bender hobbled over. As Darby entered the building, Bender called after him, "We stacked some trash in front of the hole, but you shouldn't have any issues clearing it out."

"Got it," Darby replied and disappeared inside.

Bender tried not to grimace, but his injuries weren't insignificant, and they were getting worse with each passing moment. Clotted red blood coated his upper thigh, the material around the wound shredded. Sweat beaded his brow. He was trying to will it away, but it would catch up with him soon enough. I hoped, for his sake, that when it did, it would be when it was his turn to get in the machine.

"Getting him out of the backseat isn't going to be easy," I said as I crawled inside. These crafts weren't designed with the back passengers in mind. Riders had to climb through the seats in front, as there were no doors leading to the back.

I made my way through the gap, straddling Lockland, reaching down to wrap my arms around his shoulders. As I lifted him up, he gave a sharp cry, but didn't wake. I settled him back down, deciding on a different option, and moved toward his legs to shift them to the side. I ignored his whimpers, which was devastating, but I had no choice.

Finally, I maneuvered his feet through the space between the seats where Bender was waiting. Once Bender had a firm grip on them, I slid my body under Lockland's torso, bracing his head and shoulders in my lap. Then I nodded. "He needs to go up and over first, or his body won't fit through the seats. Then out."

I don't know how we did it, but we managed to haul him out of the craft and into the building where Darby was dutifully waiting with the medi-pod door open. He'd graciously cleared it of the skeleton we'd found inside, which probably hadn't been easy for him. We laid Lockland inside. I stepped back and realized the thing wasn't running.

"What's the holdup?" I asked, making my way around to the back where Darby sat next to the liquid-hydrogen tank. A loud noise sounded from over the pod. I poked my head up to see Bender had collapsed against the wall, dispersing a pile of bones. "You okay?" I asked Bender.

He grunted, "Never better."

I crouched next to Darby. "What's wrong? Why won't this thing start?"

"I don't know. Everything seems to be in order," Darby said. "I checked and double-checked. But the on switch is not engaging this power module."

"Are you sure it's all connected? It's been a long time since this thing was up and running." I leaned forward, running my hands along the tank. Everything felt cool to the touch. At the head, where it was attached to the pod, I felt for the connections. Without them, none of this would work. My finger tweaked a lone wire that had separated from the pack. I plucked my ultra-light out of my pocket and clicked it on, positioning it next to me. I had to squint for a few moments to get my eyes used to the brightness. Then I stuck my head inside as far as it would go, grabbing the wire. It had the connector lug attached to the end, which was a relief. I couldn't see the housing without ripping the entire thing apart, so I used my teeth to pull off my glove and then felt with my bare hand where to insert it. Once I located the terminal, it snapped cleanly into place.

"Okay." I sat back, hoping with all my might that it would work. "Hit the power button."

Darby hurried around to the front, and three seconds later, the thing jumped to life like a barely restrained rocket. The motor was so powerful, the thing began to rattle the entire room, bones and all. Lights swirled and blinked on the machine, multiple beeps sounded at once, and purple ultraviolet light shot everywhere.

This thing made the medi-pod in the barracks look like a toy.

I stood, backing up a few feet, watching Darby work. He lowered the lid and pressed a few buttons, his eyes locked on the readout. "He should probably be naked for this," Darby said. "But there's no time. I'm choosing *Hyper-Triage*. It looks like it's for emergencies." He punched the button, and the entire medi-pod went black, powering down for a few short seconds, before sputtering back to life, the outside shell beginning to whir like a turbine.

It was an impressive piece of machinery.

Too bad it hadn't been designed to help Mary. But I was more than thankful it could help Lockland.

I headed toward Bender. There was nothing left to do but wait. I cleared more of the bones out of the way and sat. "What can I do for you?" I asked. "We should probably try to stop the bleeding." I gestured at his leg, then patted my vest to see what supplies I had in there. I always carried a few necessary medical supplies on me.

He shook his stubborn head, which was braced against the wall, rocking it back and forth slowly, his eyes closed. "Leave it. I'll be in there soon enough. It just hurts to breathe."

"It shouldn't be too long," I assured him, pulling out a tranq dart. "Everybody's going to be fine."

"Why in the hell do these guys want to kill themselves?" Bender murmured, his tone quieter than I was used to. "It doesn't add up. All we have in this world is survival. When you're dead, you won't give a fuck about what you left behind."

He was right. We fought for the things we needed while we were here, and when we were gone—the beauty was you no longer had to care.

"I don't know, but I'm sure we're going to find out eventually," I said, using my teeth to tug the cap off the dart. "These guys must have a long-term strategy. If the bureau's been around for more than twenty years, based on when Roman started working for them, they certainly have a plan. It pisses me off we don't know what it is, but we're close to discovering their secrets." As soon as we could give the asshole that crashed the craft some Babble. "The better question is, how could a group like this operate in our city for so long without us knowing?"

I turned to the side, positioning myself at the best angle.

Bender opened a single eye, his arms wrapped tightly in front of his chest. "What are you doing—"

"I'm tranqing you," I said, bringing the dart down before he could object or intercede. "It's for your own good." The tip entered his shoulder, and he let out a roar worthy of recognition.

"The *fuck*, Holly? I said leave it be!" He reached for the dart, which I'd left in for good measure, and yanked it out, tossing it across the room. But the deed was done. These darts were made for immediate absorption. The dosing was nominal, but the effect was nearly instantaneous.

"When have you ever known me to leave something be?" I told him as I braced my body against his, taking his weight as he began to sag.

His words came out slow and slurred. "For once…in your life…it would be nice…if you…just…"

I eased him gently to the floor, having no choice but to disrupt even more bones to make room. They cracked together ominously. "What, Bender? If I just listened like a good girl? How would that benefit you?

Now you're not in pain. And if I have any say, it will be your turn in the medi-pod before you wake up." I stood. Darby stared at me, openmouthed. "You, too?"

He turned, busying himself with the medi-pod. "No, it's not that. You did the right thing. But he's—"

"A scary monster when he's angry? I'll deal with that later. I spent the latter half of my childhood and my teen years with him. I've dealt with it all. He'll get over it…eventually. If we can get him into the medi-pod *before* he wakes up, it won't be an issue. But right now, I need something to stop his bleeding."

If he woke up before he was in the medi-pod, things would get a little dicey.

Chapter 16

It felt like hours had passed, but it'd been less than one when the machine finally let out a long beep and the turbine slowed. Bender was still out cold.

Both Darby and I jumped up.

I made it to the pod first. Words filled the small screen in front of us. But one in particular jumped out. I allowed myself to exhale, tapping my finger on the readout. "Look, it says stabilized. He's going to be okay."

Darby gently nudged me out of the way and examined the details. After a moment, he said, "The bleeding has stopped, but according to this, he has a long way to go. Apparently, hyper-triage attends to the most pressing injuries during the diagnostic phase if the patient is critical, which he was. But it leaves the rest for a more comprehensive healing process."

"Okay," I said, glancing over my shoulder. "What about Bender? Should we give him a hyper-triage, too, and then switch them again? I bet his diagnosis time won't be as long because his injuries are less severe. It'll probably help with his quadriceps and lessen the chest pain."

Darby leaned over the panel again, pressing a few buttons. "We can probably do that. Lockland is no longer in danger of dying, but his injuries are still severe—more severe than Bender's. There's no more internal bleeding. His femur bone and sternum have begun to knit back together. The concussion is now mild. But it's going to take longer for him to heal completely."

"Lockland would want Bender to take a turn," I said, making up my mind. "Let's transfer them and go from there."

Darby and I got to work, lifting Lockland out and settling Bender inside. The big guy was twice as heavy as Lockland, even though he wasn't twice the size.

Once in the pod, Bender began to moan.

I settled a hand over his chest. "You're in the medi-pod now," I told him. "Stay still. When you wake up, most of the pain will be gone." I stepped back, and Darby closed the lid, hitting the *Hyper-Triage* button. The outer shell began to crank up, just as it had for Lockland. I'd never been more thankful for anything in my entire life.

Once it was operating smoothly, I knelt by Lockland. To my surprise, he began to wake. I scooted closer, bracing my hands lightly on his shoulders. He would be disoriented when he woke. I wanted to minimize his movement. "You're okay," I murmured. "You were in a crash and sustained major injuries, but we got you to the medi-pod in time. I know it still hurts, but you're going back in soon."

He blinked, frowning. His head swiveled from side to side as he took in our location. Then he brought a hand up and rubbed it over his face. "What? I don't understand. Where's the guy?"

"The guy is with Case. We don't think he was hurt very badly. But you were, and so was Bender. You were the more critical of the two, so you went into the pod first. We just lifted you out." The floor vibrated as the medi-pod continued its full turbine spin. "Look over there." I gestured toward the machine. "Bender's inside. I know you're still hurting, but you're not going to die." Lockland tried to raise his head, but I shook mine. "Don't move. You're stabilized, but not fully healed. I'm sorry if you're in pain."

It took Lockland a few more moments to process my words. When he was ready, he said, "My craft went down?"

I nodded. "Yes, and unfortunately, I don't think Rose can be repaired. The damage to the front was too severe."

"How did it happen?"

"We don't know yet," I said. "But Darby thinks the guy you were transporting might've had some tech on him that messed with your motors. It seems he was more than willing to die."

"I remember," Lockland said. "It's coming back to me. He was laughing."

"That's what Bender said."

At the mention of Bender's name, Lockland turned toward the medi-pod. "Is he going to be okay?"

My hand remained on his shoulder, trying to keep him still. "Yes." My voice carried enough confidence for Lockland to relax beneath my grasp. "Like I said, his injuries were less severe than yours. He was in a lot of pain, so I tranqed him. Darby and I figured it was better to get him on the path to healing before you went back in."

Darby came over and crouched next to Lockland's head. "I need to take a look at your pupils. You had a massive concussion. It's been downgraded to mild, but I want to check you out." Lockland nodded, and Darby took out a light and proceeded to examine him. "The fact that you're lucid is a good sign. Are you in pain?"

Lockland's jaw was tight. "Yes."

"We're sorry about that," Darby said. "It shouldn't be too long. Bender's injuries weren't as bad."

"I'm glad he's in there," Lockland said. "Just as long as we still have that guy in our possession, it's worth it."

I quickly explained what had happened at the Emporium and that we had the Babble. "I had no choice but to leave Case and Daze outside Port Station. Four was a tough squeeze, seven was impossible. Daze has Maisie. She'll be able to warn them if anyone is coming. I'm sure they'll be fine." They'd better be.

"Did you find any of Dixon's stuff?" Lockland asked.

I glanced at Darby, who replied, "No luck on that, but we got the tech table working. It contains an incredible interactive hologram map of the city. We were able to find the room where we think the government medi-pod is located, according to Roman's tracker. Inside, we found three doors, one that leads to a zoom tunnel—"

"A zoom tunnel near our underground space by Government Square," I interrupted. Darby gave me a look. "Sorry, go on."

"Holly is correct," he continued. "By my calculations, our underground safe house is less than a quarter kilometer from our destination. Even if it's blocked by debris, we might be able to create a hole large enough to get through."

Lockland's head angled toward the ceiling as he took in what we were saying. "That's good. Getting in through the basement will keep us under the radar."

I nodded. "When we dose the bureau guy with Babble, the information we gather will help us formulate a plan. I'm anxious to understand what's going on."

A loud buzzing noise came from above the building.

It was definitely props, but they were the loudest ones I'd ever heard. I jumped up, drawing my weapons, and started to run. "Darby, stay here. Block the hole behind me and grab Lockland's Blaster. Shoot anyone who comes through that you don't recognize. Do not hesitate. Do you understand?"

"Yes," he replied.

At the hole, I turned back. "You can do this." He nodded as I ducked through the opening, jogging toward a staircase that would take me to the roof.

The props were louder now. Whoever it was would be in the vicinity within moments. I'd been on the higher floors when we first inspected the building, but not the roof. Half of it was caved in, so that part wasn't an option.

The stairway I'd chosen had a break in the ceiling on the top floor—more like a gaping hole. There was enough debris piled on the floor for me to climb up and see out. Seven was parked in plain view somewhere below me, so anyone flying over would be able to see her. Our location was compromised, no matter what. But from here, at least, I could see what was coming and how many they were.

From the noise, there was more than one.

The trash was shaky under my weight, but held. I popped my head out of the hole, glancing up. A huge craft roared toward me, the propulsion crazy loud. It was easily four times bigger than an average craft.

As it approached, it slowed.

Then I recognized it. The mover drone from Port Station.

I'd never seen its underbelly, but the coloring up top was unmistakable, as was the size. As far as I knew, that mover drone was the only one around.

Case had managed to steal the damn drone.

Either that, or the guards at Port Station had tracked us down north of the city, which was highly unlikely.

Shaking my head, I jumped down and rushed down the stairs. I made it out front right as Case landed the drone. Daze was in the passenger seat, bouncing up and down, the windshield wide enough for me to see his excitement clearly. Peering into the back, I noticed the man Lockland and Bender had taken. His head was slumped to the side. I assumed that meant he was unconscious, which would be the safest way to transport him until we figured out how he'd managed to down Lockland's craft.

The props stilled, and everything quieted.

Both doors opened with big whooshing sounds. I wondered what it was like to fly a craft that big. I'd get a chance to find out fairly quickly.

Daze hopped out, racing toward me. "We did it! We did it!"

My arms were crossed as I smiled. "I see that."

Case exited the craft and opened a secondary door. The mover drone had a door for back passengers. The first I'd ever seen. He pivoted the bureau guy out by his ankles, then hoisted him effortlessly over one shoulder. The man's head and arms lolled around lifelessly. I assumed he wasn't dead, or Case wouldn't have bothered.

Daze came rushing up the stairs, crashing into me, something I was getting used to, his skinny arms wrapping around my waist. "You should've seen Case. Maisie helped. She told us how many guards were there. But Case was so calm." His words came out in a rush as he continued, "He went in there with his Pulse up and told those guys what was going to happen, and then it happened!"

I draped my arm around the kid's shoulders, guiding him inside, heading down the hallway, Case a few meters behind. "I'm going to need more of an explanation than *it happened*." Darby had barricaded the hole, just as I'd instructed, but there were several gaps. "Darby, it's us," I called. "It was Case and Daze in the mover drone."

Darby's face appeared in front of one of the areas not covered by trash. "That's a relief," he said as he started clearing debris away from his side. Daze and I worked on our side.

The medi-pod was still spinning with Bender inside. Lockland was on the ground where I'd left him, but he looked more alert.

"Case took the mover drone?" Lockland asked.

Behind me, Case entered, dumping the bureau guy on the floor with a loud *thunk*. "Yes," he said. "We needed a craft, and it was the closest one I could find."

"Daze said you told the guards what was going to happen, and then it happened. Care to elaborate?" I asked, grinning.

"That's pretty close to the truth," he relayed. "They remembered me and my Pulse from when we took Luce. Nobody wanted any problems. There were only three guards. I told them I was going to take the craft, but that I would bring it back if they cooperated, and they'd get a loan of an E-unit for their troubles." He shrugged. "So far, so good. Maisie didn't detect anyone coming after us."

From Daze's pocket, Maisie agreed. "There are no unidentified crafts in the area. I detect multiple injuries. Lockland. Noncritical. Vitals stable. Bender. Noncritical. Vitals improving. Medi-pod power at thirty-five kilowatts. Impressive."

My eyebrows rose. "Did you just compliment the medi-pod's strength, Maisie?"

"Yes," Maisie answered as Daze pulled her out of his pocket. "Database scanned. Only one medi-pod found with more power. Recognition worthy of being exemplified."

The medi-pod began to slow.

We all glanced at it as the turbine ceased spinning. "Just so everyone knows," I said, moving toward the machine, "I tranqed Bender against his will, and he's probably going to be a little upset. I have zero regrets. He aggravated his injuries trying to get Lockland in here and was in a lot of pain. I was happy to put him out of his misery."

Once the medi-pod came to a full stop, Darby read the output data aloud. "'Quadriceps semitendinosus nominal. Hemostasis complete. Rib fracture knit. Esophageal puncture magna-sutured. Patient must re-enter within twenty-four hours to complete healing.' Sounds like he's in good shape."

It was truly impressive. "That's incredible," I said. "Daze's injuries were a little worse than Bender's, but it took a week in the barracks' medi-pod to fix him completely."

Darby lifted the lid.

Bender was awake. "Do that to me again and you will suffer the consequences," he growled when he saw me, his reaction about how I'd imagined.

I smiled down at him, making sure it was big and bright. "What? Suffer a cold shoulder for a week or two?" I rested my arms against the opening. "You can't tell me you'd rather have sat there in pain, than be knocked out and come to mostly fixed."

He sat up, his brawny bicep bunched as he gripped the edge of the pod, his face nearing mine. "You had the right idea. But next time, I control where the dart goes in. You have shitty aim."

Chapter 17

Once Bender was out of the medi-pod, Case and Darby lifted Lockland back in. "Wait for me before you question him," Lockland said as we shut the lid.

I nodded. "We won't do anything until you're done," I assured him, stepping back as Darby hit the appropriate button, this one marked *Heal.* Once the medi-pod began to churn, I glanced around. "If we're going to be doing business here once Lockland is done, let's get this place set up. First thing we need is to clear out some of these bones. I wish there was an appropriate place to put them, but for now we can find some boxes. Then we have to gather chairs. It's going to be a long night." I glanced over at the man on the floor. He hadn't moved. Not so much as a twitch. I was a little suspicious. I turned to Daze. "Hand me Maisie."

The kid set her in my palm. "I'll go find some chairs," he said as he took off through the hole.

I walked over to the man, the status reader out in

front of me. "Tell me what's wrong with this human, Maisie," I said. "Be specific."

Her lights twirled around the shadowy room, multicolor dots blinking on the walls and ceiling. After a moment, she said, "Vitals noncritical. Mild concussion and contusions. Minor electrical burns. His pulse rate is steadily increasing due to your proximity. Brain output indicates he's conscious."

"So, you're telling us this asshole is awake?" I asked, jamming the tip of my boot into his side to force him over.

"Yes, this asshole is awake," she replied in her smooth, unaffected cadence.

Falling in love with a polymer egg—seemingly unlikely before—was now a reality. She really got me.

The man rolled over with a grunt. I bent down, refraining from drawing a weapon. Case and Bender stood behind me, their firepower at the ready. Slowly, the guy opened his eyes. I noted immediately that there was no fear in them.

Instead of talking to him and giving him the pleasure of sneering, I directed my next question at Maisie. "Conduct a full-body scan of this conscious asshole who's pretending he doesn't give a shit. We're searching for any sort of tech that could render a craft inoperable. Whatever it is, it's going to be small. Then scan for any unusual weapons, including inert objects like polymers or any bio-product that doesn't contain his DNA." I watched as the man's expression dimmed. "Yeah, I figured you wouldn't like that." I stood, barely stopping myself from pressing my boot onto his chest while I waited for Maisie to make her assessments.

It didn't take her long. "Tech identified in the form of a cerulean ball."

"What's that?" I asked. I glanced over my shoulder, and both Bender and Case shook their heads. None of us had heard of one before.

"Cerulean balls are highly specialized military weapons. They produce a magnetic pulse specifically directed at motor control circuitry. To activate a pulse, one must only engage the dual magnets."

"Anything else?"

"Yes," she answered. "The cerulean ball is subdermal, located on the left forearm. Also detected is a biohazard in the form of a capsule. Once taken internally, it will stop all bodily functions within thirty seconds."

Daze came through the hole at that moment, dragging two chairs behind him.

Perfect timing.

I drew my Gem and hauled the guy off the floor, placing the cold barrel against his temple and forcing him backward onto one of the seats. "Each of you grab an arm," I directed Case and Bender. Bender held the guy's left forearm, yanking up his shirt sleeve. I holstered my Gem and withdrew the knife I kept strapped to my thigh.

"I see it," Bender said. "There's a scar and a slight pitch right here."

I nodded, moving my blade toward the destination. Once the tip was within a few centimeters of the target, the man began to thrash, bringing his legs up to try to kick me away. I'd anticipated his move, knowing he wouldn't let me do this without a fight.

With a flick of my wrist, I relocated the knife tip under his chin, causing him to recoil to avoid being pricked by the blade. "What's your name?" He gritted his teeth, eyes furious. "What are you doing with a kill pill? If things get too heavy, you'll just pop it in and take care of things? Why?" His eyes were wild, but he stayed silent. I grinned, enjoying his confusion. "Guess what? It doesn't matter if you respond. We're going to get the answers we need soon enough. In the meantime, I hope you enjoy this." I reached into my pocket and pulled out a dart, ramming a dose of Quell deeply into his thigh. Quell, developed by Walt down South, caused the recipient to float in and out of consciousness, keeping them in an unaware state.

"Damn," Bender muttered. "For future reference, you don't need to insert the entire dart into the body. The tip is enough."

I shot him a look. "Are you critiquing my dart-injecting skills?"

"Just looking out for those of us within your proximity."

The guy in the chair slumped forward, moaning lightly. We had to wait for Lockland before we could interrogate him, so it was better that he was out of it. I wasn't interested in discovering any more tricks or death wishes he had, and it was clear he wasn't going to talk until he got Babble.

Using the edge of the blade, I bent over his forearm and popped the cerulean ball out. It rolled in the middle of my palm, covered in blood and goo. I cleaned my knife on my thigh before sheathing it. Then I picked up the ball between my thumb and index finger. It had a small gap in the middle, and blood eased out of the crevasse, dripping down my fingers.

With effort, I compressed the two sides together, forcing the gap to close.

The effects were immediate. The medi-pod began to slow, and the lights began to flicker. I let go. Things resumed. I whistled. "That is a powerful magnetic pulse," I said. "And all this guy had to do was pinch this together under his skin."

Bender held out his hand, and I dropped the ball into his palm. He brought the thing up to his eye to study it. "This will definitely come in handy later."

The guy in the chair made a few gurgling sounds, his eyes rolling back in his head as saliva dripped down his chin. He wasn't making any sudden movements, so that was fine with me. I grinned. "Little does this bastard know he's about to reveal all his secrets to us."

"Yeah," Bender said. "But now we're going to have to wait for him to recover from that shit before he talks."

"The amount in that dart lasts about an hour. I'm not worried," I said. "We have to wait for Lockland to get out of the pod anyway. Let's find that kill pill Maisie said he had on him and make sure we check him thoroughly, including inside his mouth. Maisie may have missed something. The tech is high military grade. Stuff that would've been rounded up immediately following the meteor strike and obviously kept under wraps."

Case rummaged through one of the guy's pockets. "Found it." He held up a pill the color of the sky on my wall screen as Daze dragged a few more chairs into the room. The kid was making himself useful.

Darby came forward, and Case handed it over. Darby held it up to his nose and sniffed.

"Does it have a scent?" I asked.

Darby nodded. "Slightly acidic with a sour undertone. I've studied these before. Blue is the worst. It contains a chemical that instantly neutralizes certain atomic bonds. Everything in your body just stops working."

"This guy doesn't look that old," I said. "I was expecting someone in Dixon's age group, fifties or sixties. He looks like he's in his thirties at most. That means they have to be actively recruiting if they've been around for as long as we think they have." Roman's notes indicated that the medi-pod project he'd been working on had been going on for years before he joined. He'd been down South for ten, so that meant the group started at least twenty, if not thirty, years ago. This guy would've been a little kid.

Case stood over the drooling guy. "The more I'm looking at him, the more he seems familiar."

I inclined my head. "Was he in your former militia group? Someone who was out on a mission the day Dixon killed everybody?"

"No," he replied with certainty. "But Dixon probably had dealings with him at some point. Sometimes I caught a glimpse of who he met with from afar. If I had to guess, he's from the big militia down South, the powerful one trying to round up the tribes. If he is part of that group, we've got bigger trouble to deal with than just the Bureau of Truth. That means their scope is much, much larger than we thought." Case didn't have to stress the implications. If the bureau was connected to the powerful militia we'd encountered on our journey down South, it would be a hell of a mess.

Daze, done with the chairs, dragged in a large metal box he'd found. He stood next to it, staring at the bones on the floor. I walked over, settling a hand on his shoulder. "I'd like to believe these women were missed and someone loved them."

He nodded. "Me, too."

Together, we began to carefully set bones inside. Case joined us, and we worked to clear a small area. Once that box was full, Daze dragged it out of the room without a word.

Glancing at our potential tell-all captive, I settled my arms across my chest. "Whatever comes out of his mouth is going to change us."

"I know," Bender grumbled, coming to stand next to me. "But the way I look at it, it's time for a change. We can't keep living like we have. Our resources won't hold out. We're surviving on crumbs. These guys know that." He gestured to the man in the chair.

"They've known for a long time. I have a hunch this group stayed back from The Water Initiative on purpose. Maybe they struck a deal with whoever was in charge at the time, and since then, they've been actively building their troops and getting organized. A few defectors like Dixon managed to fuck things up for a while, but they're not stopping their original plan."

"Which is?" I asked. I had my hunches, too, but I wanted to hear what he had to say.

"A new world order," Case said, answering first.

My gaze shot to his. "Possibly. But one that will be full of torture and violence. That's all these militias know how to do. Inflict pain and agony on all who don't conform to their authoritarian ways. They will massacre thousands of innocents who refuse to bend to their rule." It was disgusting to think about, and my mind immediately went to Gia. Her existence had been abysmal. She'd been repeatedly sexually assaulted and beaten and then murdered and thrown away—discarded like trash. My life could've easily ended up just like hers had I not found my family before it was too late. Life in this world was just a set of near misses.

The outskirt crossed his arms, legs splayed. "They don't care about anyone but themselves. They value their survival above all else."

"How are they going to survive? Do they have magical abilities we don't know about?" I challenged.

"I'm sure they've been hoarding resources for decades," he answered. "Whoever started this was likely in a position of power. By now, they probably have a precise calculation of how many souls they can sustain until they can build and develop new resources."

My fingers went to my temples. "This is insane. If they've been hoarding resources for that long, they could've been using them for everyone's benefit. The world would be a better place right now."

"They don't care about everyone," Case said. "I lived it. The militia organization is completely secular. They believe they're superior in both body and mind. That's why these guys are so cocky." He gestured at the man in the chair, who had begun to slowly move his head, the effects of the Quell lessening. "The ones they send on these errands are the most loyal. They've bought into their way of life and grew up working solely for the common good. Hell, he was probably born into it and knows nothing different."

"If Dixon knew about this entire organization and the link between the bureau and the militia," I said, "and tried to stop it, he could be considered a hero in some people's eyes."

Case's expression dimmed. "Dixon was no hero. He cared about no one but himself."

"That may be true," I said. "But as he was selfishly looking out for himself, he inadvertently benefited all of us by staving off this overthrow attempt until now. I don't think it's a coincidence that everything happened after he died. They probably felt like they could proceed again once he was out of their way for good."

From behind us, the medi-pod slowed.

Bender made his way over and, once it stopped, helped Lockland out. "Looks like it's time to find out what this asshole has to say. No more fucking guesses."

Chapter 18

By the time Lockland was out of the pod and organized, the bureau guy, firmly secured to the chair in front of us, began to fully wake up. We agreed he should be alert before we gave him the Babble. I'd been content to wait a little longer, even though waiting was my least favorite thing to do, mostly because the look on his face when he realized what was about to happen was going to be worth its weight in coin.

As he came to and took in his surroundings, he sputtered, "Let me…*go.*" He tested his restraints, which were rock solid, finding no give. His head came up, and he contemplated us. Five adults and one kid all sitting in a semicircle two meters away. All giving him the same *screw you* face. "You're going to perish," he growled. "If you're not going to let me go, just kill me. I welcome it."

"Yeah, about that," I said as I stood. "We're *dying* to know why you're so anxious to end your life." I moved toward him, my hands clasped behind my back. The dart, the one that previously contained Quell but was now filled with Babble, was tucked in my grasp. He didn't need to see it yet. I wasn't expecting him to answer freely, but I was interested in learning more about his temperament to better figure out how he was going to handle all this.

"I'm not scared of dying," he spat.

"That's incredibly clear," I said. "But that doesn't answer my question. I asked you *why* you are so willing to die. Do you have knowledge of a greater force waiting for you on the other side? Will the sun be shining there? Please tell us." Giving this guy a chance to proselytize might get him to talk. People who held such firm beliefs often couldn't help themselves.

"You would never understand," he said, ending on a whine.

"Give me a try," I said. "I might be a woman, but I do have a working brain where the synapses fire regularly." I gestured to my crew behind me. "And if I can't muddle it out, certainly my friends will be able to help."

"I'm not telling you anything," he said, his mouth snapping shut, then opening again quickly. "Just know that your time is near."

"I'll have to disagree with you there," I said, stopping next to him. "You are going to talk, and it just so happens I have the very thing that will compel you to comply." I brandished the dart, rolling it between my fingers in front of his face, enjoying his expression as it flittered from bafflement to apocalyptic anger in less than three seconds.

"You can't use that on me!" he sputtered, trying to kick out his legs, hoping to scuttle out of the way. Except, it didn't work because his ankles had been shackled to the chair, and the chair had been reinforced with metal braces in anticipation of lots of defensive movements.

Everything held beautifully.

Bender rose and moved to his other side. "She can, and she will," he said as he bent over the guy, his gaze narrowing. "And I have a feeling she doesn't give a shit about how far the needle goes in either. You're about to spill your guts and give us everything you have in that brain of yours." Bender flicked his finger against the man's temple. The guy shrank back, as most people did around Bender, even if they were trying to sell themselves as a cocky, self-assured pain in the ass who wasn't afraid to die.

"We know about you," the guy said through a clenched jaw. "We know about all of you." His head rotated as he peered at each of us. "You've been prancing around this city, oblivious to us, but we've been watching you for *years*."

"That was your biggest mistake," I said, jamming the dart into his neck until his skin met my fingertips. His mouth gaped open and shut, but nothing came out. "You should've been doing more than *watching* us."

Reluctantly, I slid the thing out, rubbing it on my

pants before I stuck it back in my vest. My outfit was going to need a thorough cleaning once this was over. I had enough of this guy's bodily fluids on me to warrant a biohazard bath.

The guy's eyes rolled back in his head as his muscles began to tremble. Darby rushed over, repositioning his head and looking into his eyes.

"Is that a normal reaction?" Bender asked.

Darby shrugged. "I have no idea. When I came to after I had Babble, I didn't remember anything, not even what happened before they gave it to me. His pupils are dilated, but not overly so."

"So, do we just start asking him questions?" I asked, skeptical we'd get anything out of him in this state. "He doesn't look like he's going to do much talking." Once Darby let go, the guy's head fell completely backward, his mouth gaping open, his eyes nothing but whites.

"Again," Darby said, "I'm not sure. I've never interrogated someone on Babble. I don't know how people respond."

Daze brought Maisie out. "How do we interrogate someone on Babble?" he asked the egg a few centimeters from his lips, which was his preference.

"An injection of the drug called Truth Serum 241, nicknamed Babble, will produce effects immediately," she intoned. "The injected should be seated in a comfortable, conversational position, facing the interrogator. If needed, cold water can be used to counter sluggish behavior."

Bender grabbed the guy's head and pushed it forward. It fell limply, toward his lap. "We should've used a chair with a headrest," he said.

"I'm pretty sure one doesn't exist around here." I glanced at Daze. "There's a jug of water in the back of Seven. Go grab it." Nodding, he shoved Maisie in his pocket and took off.

"If we take him out of the chair, we lose the restraints," Lockland said, trying to hide a grimace. Upon exiting the medi-pod, he'd claimed he felt fine, but I could tell he was in pain. The data readout on his condition had stated that he'd need at least one more run before he was healed enough to move around. But he'd insisted we get on with the interrogation.

"Let's slide his chair against the wall," I suggested. "That will provide him with an adequate headrest." I leaned over and tugged out the two metal rods that served as braces for the chair. Bender and I both grabbed the chair legs and slid it and the guy backward. "That should do the trick." I positioned the metal rods against the front to give the chair some stability if he tried to use his head as leverage. But, honestly, he didn't look like he was in any shape to act out. We would likely be fine.

Daze brought in the water. I took the jug and proceeded to splash a hefty dose into the guy's face. He sputtered and coughed, shaking off the haze of the drug, just as Maisie had predicted he would.

I bent over to gauge his expression. It was slack, showing no emotion.

"What's your name?" I asked.

"Reed," he answered readily, no hesitation.

Darby and Case moved our chairs forward, while Bender helped Lockland relocate closer so everyone had a front-row view. "Where are you from, Reed?" I asked as I sat. I was going to ask the first few questions, but we'd all agreed to interject as needed. We had enough Babble, so there was no worry about timing. None of us was leaving this room until we were satisfied.

"Militia base S17," he answered. His voice reminded me of Maisie's monotone, but with a more human cadence.

"Where exactly is militia base S17 located?" I asked.

"Approximately three and a half hours south of here," he answered.

"Is your militia base the biggest one south of the city?"

"Yes." So he was from the big base we'd flown over that Case had been worried about.

"How did you get here?" Lockland asked.

"By craft."

"Did you come alone?" Bender asked.

"No. There were three of us."

"What was your mission?" Case asked.

"To take down the adversaries who threaten our agenda," Reed replied.

"And who exactly are those adversaries?" I asked, knowing full well he was referring to us.

"A group in the city with increased power."

"Does this group have a name?" I asked.

"We call them Bender's crew."

I chuckled. "I forgot to tell you," I said, addressing Bender. "The guys we ran into who were hired to do surveillance at the Emporium called us Bender's crew, too. Did you know that's how people referred to us?"

"Yeah," Bender said, scratching the back of his neck. "But I never paid much attention to it. I don't give a shit what other people think."

"Works for me," I said, returning my attention to Reed. "Reed, why does Bender's crew pose a threat to your group?"

"Because they fight to protect defective humans," Reed answered.

"And you don't protect defective humans?" I asked.

"No," he said. "Defective humans deserve to die."

"Why do they deserve to die?" Darby asked.

"Because they are weak," Reed said. "They will die anyway, so it doesn't matter. We must populate a new race. One that can last."

"Last for what?" I asked.

"They will come," Reed said.

"Who's coming?" I asked, genuinely puzzled.

"The Flotilla will return. They will bring us new hope, and we will provide them with a new population."

"How long have you known this?" I asked.

"It has always been known," he answered.

"Were you born into this militia?" Case asked.

"Yes," he said.

"What is the Bureau of Truth?" Lockland asked. It was the big question we all wanted an answer to.

"We have infiltrated the government," Reed said. This time, there was a little infusion of glee in his voice, like the response to this question was hardwired with happiness. "They do not know what lies beneath their very noses."

That sounded like a quote of some kind, maybe a common militia mantra. "Where did that saying come from?" I asked.

"My father," Reed said. "The time draws near for us to regain our power."

"Also a quote from your father?" I asked. "What was his name?"

"Yes. Jonas."

"Is he still alive?" I asked.

"No."

"Did he start the militia after The Water Initiative left town?" Lockland asked.

"No."

"So, the militia was already active before The Water Initiative?" I asked.

"Yes."

"Did your group make a pact with the former government about The Water Initiative?" Case asked.

"We have become the government," Reed answered.

That couldn't be completely true, because Claire had worked for the government for years and hadn't known about the Bureau of Truth until recently. She would've known if the entire government was being secretly run by a militia down South. That information would've bubbled to the surface at some point.

"Our questions are too broad," I said. "We need to ask him specific questions in order to gain the right information. There's a good chance Reed doesn't know everything. He was clearly born into it, and his dad might've played a prominent role, but he might not hold the answers."

"He has enough in his brain to give us a good idea," Lockland said. "The Flotilla leaving seems to have been a turning point for this group. But I agree, our questions need to be more focused." Lockland rearranged his chair, but not without making a face. We needed to get him back into the medi-pod as soon as possible. "What is the mission of the Bureau of Truth?"

"To eradicate."

Chapter 19

Eradication was contrary to what the government was supposed to do for its people. "To eradicate whom?" I asked.

"Any and all who stand in our way," Reed answered.

In an effort to redirect, I asked, "Other than to kill everyone you don't like, what is the Bureau of Truth's mission?"

"To control the city and repopulate it."

"Why are the people here defective?" I asked.

"They do not follow our ways."

"What are the ways of militia S17?" Case asked.

"We are the strongest and smartest. We alone know what lies ahead."

"What lies ahead?" Darby asked.

"Salvation."

A clearer picture was beginning to emerge. According to what I knew of history, several groups after the dark days had believed that the meteor strike was delivered as divine punishment for the human inhabitants of Earth. That the people had sinned and had somehow deserved their fate. These groups had billed it as a mass cleansing. I'd never understood how anyone could believe such a thing, and it surprised me that sixty years later, people were still embracing such a notion.

I got off my chair, unable to sit still any longer. "So, once you cleanse the population of defective humans and bring in your own people, the true believers of your cause, you will achieve salvation?"

"Once the Flotilla returns, we will merge in a rebirth, ushering this world into a new era. Only then will we achieve salvation."

"And this is a cause worth dying for?" Case asked.

"Of course," Reed answered.

"What does the world look like once salvation is achieved?" Lockland asked.

"The sun will shine again, the water will recede, vegetation will return, animals will thrive and multiply. We will be in the good graces of the Spirit Advisor once again." His tone was absolute. He believed what he was saying with his entire being.

I glanced around the group. "It seems Reed's militia has something in common with the Sun Optimists." I met Case's gaze, which was stony. "If they follow the rules, amass an army, hoard resources, and kill off all the lowly deviants who don't buy into their way of thinking, the sun will shine again, and there will be rebirth and salvation. Please correct me if I'm on the wrong track."

"That's what he is saying, on a basic level," Lockland replied. "Or at least that's how it started more than thirty years ago. But it would be foolish not to factor in power, greed, and the inherent quest to control one's destiny. That's at the root of this. The original concept might've started from a place of ideological intent—that if they adhered to some strict rules, they could alter the world for the better, and that's certainly what they regurgitate to their followers. But over the years, based on what you and Case saw firsthand down South, it's morphed into something darker. After the meteor strike, don't forget, many small factions formed, including the Sun Optimists. They believe that they will be blessed with a change in our environment if they work hard enough for it. But as far as I know, it never turned darker than that. Then there are the Iron Worshipers, who feel the world has been blessed by iron and refuse anything not made from their sacred material. Again, I don't believe they've developed a quest to give birth to a new race. So, as this Bureau of Truth group might have started similarly, it's changed dramatically over the years, likely only holding on to a few of the tenets of the original mission. The rest is made up of power and greed."

"Don't forget the Meteor Fellowship," Bender grunted. "They believe we're being punished, left here to rot in this hellscape for the sins our ancestors committed, and actively hope we get wiped out by another meteor." He shook his head. The shared feeling by all of us when we thought of such groups and their crazy belief systems. "But overall they're harmless. Definitely not trying to wipe out the population. After all, why bother to do something a meteor can take care of in a few seconds?"

I felt like pacing, so in an effort to keep still, I leaned my shoulder against the wall. Since we weren't asking questions, Reed remained quiet. "I realize groups like those exist," I said. "But they've always included a very small segment of our population. Isolated belief systems haven't gained traction, for the most part, because their followers are considered loonies that should know better but somehow don't. So somehow, this Bureau of Truth group managed to gain incredible traction, infiltrating the government with the agenda to kill the masses, save for their followers, and have kept it a secret for thirty years. It's hard for me to believe something like that could've grown to wield so much control."

"Once you understand the inner workings of such a group," Case said, "it's not that hard to conceive it could happen."

I raised my eyebrows in his direction. "Please explain," I encouraged.

"Well," Case said, "if the person they decided to follow was incredibly charismatic and had a solid vision, you'd be surprised how quickly the disenfranchised sign on. If whoever started this targeted militias and people with power to begin with, then control was easily within their grasp in a short period of time. Then, before they knew it, their followers conformed to a specific way of thinking without even realizing it."

"How could they not realize it?" I asked.

"Because life here is desperate," Case answered. "They *want* to believe. If they buy into the concept that this group will change their life for the better, and that is reinforced daily, they will continue to believe even when faced with incredible adversity."

"At some point, you'd think they'd figure out that the group doesn't have their best interests at heart," I said.

Case shook his head. "Very few ever change their minds. For example, the Sun Optimist belief system was started by a man my sustainer parents described as 'enchanting' and 'godlike.' When they talked about him, their voices grew low and they became reverent. We said a prayer in his name, Gustaf Lorrey, every single night, and he'd been dead for twenty years by that time. So even then, he controlled them. If another Sun Optimist claimed tomorrow that they'd unearthed notes written by this man and that those writings stated they were supposed to jump into the sea on a specific date in the future, they would. His power hasn't faded for them. It's the opposite. They ache for it. They want what he promised. They've been conditioned for it, and they will not be persuaded otherwise."

I pondered what Case was telling us from firsthand experience. "So, essentially," I said, "you're saying there's a possibility that whoever started the Bureau of Truth and is responsible for strengthening the S17 militia could be someone so charismatic that, even if they've been dead for years, their presence still motivates people like Reed and the guy I killed at the Emporium to keep doing their bidding?"

"Yes, that's exactly what I'm saying," Case said. "This guy"—he gestured at Reed—"was born into a group in which his father likely played a key role. It makes total sense he would be willing to die for his cause. It's the only thing he knows. For him, there's nothing else."

Lockland stood on shaky legs. I made an instinctive move to help, but stopped short. It was his choice if he wanted to be up and around. "I agree with you," Lockland told Case. "In order to keep their secret for as long as they did, they had to have been fanatical, with only a very few breaking free, like Dixon. Dixon knew what their end goal was and made it harder for them to achieve it."

"Dixon cared about Dixon," Case stated. "He may have killed the militia I was involved with to ultimately lessen the growing numbers of S17, but he was after their resources and nothing more. He spared me because he realized I didn't buy into anyone else's belief system, but mostly because he needed an ally he could control, and he chose right." Case was admonishing himself by voicing his regret about the role he played in allowing Dixon to exercise control over him.

"Yeah, he chose right until it killed him," I retorted, pinning Case with a look, daring him to challenge me. He'd been a young man at the time Dixon showed up. One who'd been abused for years, grateful for a way out.

"Dixon got what he deserved," Bender said. "End of story. I don't care if he was actively working against S17. He didn't do enough, and it's up to us to finish the task."

"To do that," I said, "we have to keep questioning this guy." I jerked my thumb toward Reed, who seemed to be tracking our conversation, but unless he was asked a direct question, he was content to stay silent.

Lockland limped over to Reed, bracing his hand against the wall above the guy's head. "Was Perseus Leavenworth your leader?"

Perseus Leavenworth was the very first acting president after the dark days. Our last official president, Alphonse Guerrero, had left with the Flotilla. There had been two others in between, but they'd been in office only a short time and had done nothing noteworthy. As the stories went, people had gravitated toward Perseus because he'd been gregarious and energetic. He'd led a solid initiative to try to knit the city back together, but he died only a few years into his tenure when a piece of falling debris landed on his head.

"No," Reed answered.

"Who was your first leader?" Lockland asked.

"Brock Shannon."

Lockland's gaze snapped to mine. We all knew Brock Shannon. He was notorious in our short post-meteor history, being the first person tried for murder after the dark days. He'd been accused of flaying bodies and displaying them in front of his residence for all to see, spouting gibberish about people coming back from the dead in reanimated corpses to devour the remaining population by eating their flesh.

It was said he'd lost his mind and had been killed for his crimes.

"Brock Shannon was jailed and sentenced to death for the murder of at least thirty people over fifty years ago," Lockland said. "How can he be your leader?"

Reed shook his head. "They jailed the wrong man. Brock escaped."

"Is Brock still alive?" I asked.

"I don't know."

"Elaborate," I ordered.

"He speaks to us through his special army."

This was getting weirder by the second. With a single eyebrow cocked, I glanced around the group. "How many here think Brock is dead and gone and probably has been for a long time?"

Lockland made his way back to his seat. "Building on what Case was saying earlier, Brock could've easily been the figurehead needed to start this movement. Someone notorious and well-known. Someone who would garner specific attention. He didn't even have to be alive. Pretending he was might've been enough."

"Reed, who are the members in Brock Shannon's special army?" I asked Reed.

"Their leader is Tillman," he answered.

"I know who that is," Case said. "He visited my militia a few times, and I'm fairly certain Dixon had dealings with him. He's a mean SOB, and most of us pretended to be busy with anything we could find whenever he arrived."

"If Dixon had dealings with him *after* Dixon defected from the Bureau of Truth, that complicates things," I said. "Could you pick him out of a crowd? Do you know what he looks like?"

Instead of Case, Reed answered, "He has dark hair, cut closely, silvered with gray. He stands thirty centimeters taller than me and will shoot you if you don't cooperate. If you step out of line, he will punish you. That punishment will cause lasting pain."

I crossed my arms. Tillman sounded lovely. "Tillman could be the guy we're looking for, the one who's behind this chaos. I have to admit, it's pretty evil genius to use someone like Brock Shannon to get a bunch of militants to listen to you. Nothing gets crazy's attention like other crazy."

Darby came off his chair. By the cant of his head, he'd been in deep thought, trying to puzzle everything out. "What's still unexplained is why they waited so long," Darby muttered. "If they had all these resources, guns, and access to tech we don't have, like UACs that send and receive live video, why would they wait so many years to strike? Brock

Shannon was executed over fifty years ago. That's an incredibly long time for a group to wait to implement their agenda."

I shrugged. "I agree with you. Ask Reed."

I moved aside, and Darby took my place. "Reed, why have you waited so long to take over the city?"

"The time wasn't right."

"What reasons were you given for why the time wasn't right?" Darby tried again.

"We need more people," Reed said. "Without them, we fail, just like Tandor."

That was an interesting tidbit. He'd just admitted the Bureau of Truth was connected to Tandor, proving our assumptions.

"Why did Tandor fail?" Darby asked.

"He wouldn't listen," Reed said as anger crept into his words. "We tried to control his tribe, but his group was too strong. Tillman was angry. So we made Tandor a deal. We offered him the city in exchange for his tribe."

"Except you knew he would fail, right, Reed?" I asked. "You knew he would come up against Bender's crew and he would fail."

"Yes."

"So Tillman was trying to get rid of Tandor," I said. "Send him away from his tribe, knowing he would die, so you could gather up the people he left behind and get on with repopulating the city with your followers?"

"Yes."

"It must've made Tillman mad that he couldn't get to the scientists sooner," I commented. "The scientists were a big prize, weren't they? Without them, you wouldn't have enough resources to take over the city."

"What scientists?"

Chapter 20

We spent the next ten minutes grilling Reed about the scientists, not believing he knew nothing about them, but in the end it was clear he had no idea who they were.

"That proves Teddy Candor, aka Tandor," I said to the group, "managed to keep the biggest secret from the most powerful militia around. How he achieved such a thing boggles the brain, given our short interaction with him. He didn't seem like a mastermind."

"If Tillman knew about the scientists and the resources they have," Darby said, "I assume things would've gone much differently. It's a relief he doesn't know."

"Agreed. And we have to keep it that way at all costs," I said. "It proves Tandor understood he was being played, but lucky for us, he had an abnormal amount of overconfidence in himself, with no real idea what he'd encounter when he reached the city."

Case shook his head. "I think it might've been the opposite. Tillman set Tandor up, that much is true, but I think he hoped Tandor would succeed in taking all of you down. If he had, Tillman's agenda would've been much easier. From my inside source, I know Tandor had information about all of you. He was able to track your whereabouts from the beginning. The only thing he didn't anticipate was Daze." Case tossed a look of gratitude at the kid, who'd been quietly listening to the interrogation. Daze jutted his chin out and then promptly scuffed his feet against the ground, overcome by the sudden attention, his cheeks tinting a rosy pink. "If Daze hadn't stolen the quantum drive, Tandor might've succeeded. The kid forced his hand. And if he'd been successful, Tillman would've taken over, because he has the Bureau of Truth behind him. If Tandor had known about the Bureau of Truth, and the scope of the S17 militia and their plans, he probably would've stayed down South, safe and secure with the scientists, hoarding his resources."

"This is proving to be a complicated web of deception, each side holding back valuable information." I nodded. "Reed's answers still don't explain everything, but it's a start. Using Brock Shannon's name took ingenuity. And to keep that story alive took even more. What we need right now is to find out for sure who's behind it. We're assuming it's Tillman, but we don't know for sure."

"It makes more sense why they aborted the medipod program," Lockland said. "They had no intention of saving anyone. Roman's notes mention that the medi-pod program was sponsored by someone with power, influence, and money. And after he or she died, the program went with them. Reed probably doesn't have that information. But I'm certain whoever that person was holds a key in all this."

I turned to our prisoner. "Reed, are you familiar with the medi-pod program the Bureau of Truth was responsible for?"

"Yes."

"Who started the program?"

"Brock Shannon."

"That can't be your answer for everything," I said. "Brock Shannon didn't start the medi-pod program. Who started the program?"

"Brock Shannon," Reed insisted.

"Why did he start the program?" Darby asked.

"His wife was infected by Plush. It's why he started killing seekers and placing them on stakes in front of his residence. After he escaped, he fled down South and did what he had to do to save her."

That made some sense, if in fact Brock Shannon had survived. "So Brock Shannon's original mission was to save seekers? Then when he died, they closed the program down?"

"He didn't die."

I fought my urge to pace in a small circle in front of the guy. "If Brock Shannon's still alive, then why is the medi-pod program inactive? I thought his goal was to save seekers?"

"It was deemed evil to save those who are defective," Reed said. "They destroyed all of the medi-pods."

"Are you sure about that?" I asked.

"Yes."

"Who gave the order?" I asked.

"Tillman."

"Of course he did," I said.

Darby leaned over, studying Reed's face and eyes as he asked, "Has anybody you know ever been cured of anything? Something you didn't think was possible?"

"Yes."

"Please be specific," Darby said. "What kind of ailments did they have, and when were they cured? Were they brought to the city for treatment?"

I could see where Darby was going with this and was grateful he was here. Our rapid-fire questions were producing answers, but they weren't exactly leading us in the right direction. Darby had the skills and finesse we needed.

"Yes, they were taken to the city," Reed confirmed. "Grave injuries were healed because we are on the correct path to salvation. Rewards are bountiful if you believe."

"Did the people who were cured go to the Medi Center?" Darby continued.

"No."

"Where did they go?"

"I don't know."

"I think it's pretty clear Reed is a foot soldier," I

said. "The higher-ups wouldn't share much with someone of his rank."

"According to his answers," Lockland said, "there's a good possibility they kept one of the medi-pods working to cure those in their group who needed it, just like you thought. It must be powerful in its own right, capable of doing much more than mending a seeker."

"Have you ever been inside the building that the Bureau of Truth occupies in Government Square?" Darby asked.

"Yes," Reed replied.

"How many people reside in that building?"

"Twelve members live there."

"Are you free to go anywhere in the building?" Darby asked.

"No."

"What rooms are off-limits?"

"We must remain on the main floor. There is a large meeting room and three guest rooms. The rest of the building is classified."

I bet it was.

"What are the names of the members?" Darby asked.

"I don't know."

"What you mean you don't know?" I asked. "You said you've been there and had meetings."

"He didn't say he's been to meetings," Darby clarified. "He said there's a meeting room. If they're trying to maintain their secret, as they have for thirty years, it makes sense that they would cloak the identities of the members who live and work in the city. If anything happens, and the militia is defeated, these guys can blend into the general populace without anyone ever knowing they were involved. From everything Reed's said so far, my guess is these twelve are the responsible authority. They make the decisions and communicate directly with Tillman, who then makes sure their orders are carried out. Almost like a big corporation would have operated before the dark days. These twelve would've been the top executives."

"Twelve's an okay number," Bender said. "We won't have trouble getting rid of twelve."

"Yeah," I agreed. "But they're going to have precautions in place if something goes wrong. Tillman's probably been instructed to start an all-out war on the city if something happens to them. They've had literally years and years to plan this. For all we know, they've planted doomsday bombs all over town, set to destroy with the punch of a button."

Darby said, "It would be a mistake not to be cognizant of their agenda before we strike. Holly's right. It's been in place for years. Nothing about this seems hurried. It's been methodically planned, down to brainwashing foot soldiers as children. Their willingness to wait until the timing is considered perfect speaks volumes. If we enter that building and take them out, we risk retaliation on the city itself. At this point, we have to believe they will fight fiercely to keep their power."

I sat, leaning over as I brought my hands to my face, rubbing my eyes. We all needed a little time to think and process everything we'd just heard. There had to be a solution to all this. I refused to believe there wasn't a way we could win this war.

Daze surprised me by getting out of his seat and walking up to Reed. I raised my head to watch. "Reed, do you come to the city at set times?" he asked.

"Yes."

"When?" the kid asked.

"We come once per annum."

Only once a year? That was surprising. But if they were trying to keep things a secret, that would do it. Having strange people constantly entering and exiting the city at all times would call attention to them.

"Is this your designated time to be in the city?" Daze continued.

"No."

"Why were you called here?"

"We must take care of the threat before they find out about us," Reed answered. We didn't have to guess to know who *they* were.

Too late, your secret has been exposed.

"How many people came with you?" Daze asked. The kid was good at this.

"Three."

"Was one of them Tillman?"

"No. Tillman resides twenty kilometers from the base."

"What happens if you fail?" Daze asked.

"Death. But I welcome it."

Yeah, we know that.

"If all three of you die, will they send three more?" Daze asked.

"No, Tillman will come."

I stood and made my way to the kid, settling my hand on his shoulder and giving it a squeeze, letting him know he was doing a good job. "How many will come with Tillman?" I asked, picking up Daze's thread.

"Tillman's army contains thirty men."

"How many live at the militia base?" I asked.

"One hundred seventy-six."

Lockland cleared his throat, appearing tired. We had to wrap this up soon. "How do the twelve in Government Square communicate with Tillman?"

"We have private bandwidths set up," he replied.

Damn, that was handy.

And had probably taken a lot of time to organize—like, years. Private bandwidths meant they had their own radio towers.

"Do the twelve have set schedules?" Lockland asked. "Do they all work within the government?"

"Yes. They all have government jobs."

"Do their coworkers know who they are?" I asked.

"No."

"So they blend," I said. "But people must see them coming in and out of that building."

"Not necessarily," Darby said. "Remember the hologram map? There are three entrances into the basement of that building. My guess is they utilize at least one of those exclusively. We need to get back to the barracks and study the map again. See if there's a direct route to someplace nearby where they could enter without being seen."

I nodded. "Who knows? Maybe they have a pneumatic-tube system like the Emporium does. It wouldn't be that farfetched." We wouldn't know until we got there. Reed's head dropped forward, and he began to moan. The Babble was wearing off. Lockland needed a break, so this worked fine. "I agree with Darby," I said as I bent down to unshackle Reed's legs. "We need to get back to the hologram map. We get this guy to the barracks and secure him until we dose him again. I'm all for getting the mover drone out of here as well. If Port Station changes their mind and decides to track us down, the barracks is off the radar."

"I'll stay here with Lockland until he's done in the pod," Bender said. "Then we'll follow you back." Lockland's craft was wrecked, and Bender's was back at the barracks. That left only Seven and the mover drone parked out front.

I glanced at Case, who addressed Bender. "We'll take the mover drone, since we have five. You take my craft. There are no tricks, just a standard startup."

"I can handle it." Bender nodded.

"We'll leave the hatch unlocked," Case said. "Look for the mover drone straight west of the barracks and park next to it. It's best we keep all the crafts away from our location for now."

"Will do," Bender said.

"Do you need Darby to stay?" I asked. Darby was key to deciphering the hologram map, but if Lockland needed him, that was the priority.

Lockland glanced at Darby. "Bender just has to press a button, right?"

Darby nodded. "Yes. The diagnostics are all locked in. You're patient one in the system right now. Bender is patient two."

"After Bender takes his turn, we're making one stop before we head to the barracks," Lockland said as he limped toward the machine.

"Where to?" I asked.

"We need Claire."

Chapter 21

"Where in the hell are they?" I asked. It was going on four hours since we'd arrived back with Reed, who was currently dosed up on Quell. No amount of dissuading had convinced Lockland not to go get Claire. He was right that we needed her. But taking Seven anywhere near the city was incredibly risky. "I knew I should've gone with them."

"Lockland laid out his plan," Case said. "You heard him. Claire knows how to dodge the tail if she's being followed. They also have a meeting place that no one knows about. Plus, the meet-up was planned after blackout, which gives them ample cover."

All of those things were true, but it didn't make me feel much better.

"Yeah," I said. "But from what Reed said, the Bureau of Truth is sneaky and content to wait, even if it takes years. If they've discovered Claire is part of our team, they might lie in wait for this kind of rendezvous, knowing she'll meet up with us at some point."

"I thought you always kept your connection with Claire out of the public eye," Case said.

"We did—I mean, we do," I grumbled. We'd always been careful to keep Claire at a distance, so no one would know how close she was to us. "But this was before we knew any specifics about the Bureau of Truth. Claire helped smuggle Darby out of his incarceration a short time ago, so it's feasible that they suspect her. Honestly, if I were nervous that I was about to be discovered, like the Bureau of Truth seems to be, I'd have a sharp eye on anyone and everyone."

"Come look at this," Darby called from the tech table, where he and Daze had their heads together.

As I moved in their direction, I glanced at the sleeping pod that held Reed, his arms and legs bound. We'd given him Quell because, once he'd awoken fully right after we arrived back, he'd started threatening to take his own life every five minutes. We had no idea how he would achieve such a thing, since we'd taken his weapons and his kill pill, but I didn't trust the bastard. We needed more information from his head, so we weren't willing to risk it.

I sat down on the couch next to Darby.

He pointed at the building next to the one we believed the Bureau of Truth was headquartered in. "I believe the twelve members come in through this building here. It used to be the Residence Assistance Office, the agency that once helped people set up housing and provided a few supplies. It hasn't been used as that for a long time, but I'm fairly certain there are still offices in there, and people come and go, so it would raise less suspicion." His finger trailed over a path, leaving a quickly evaporating red line. "If you head into this room, there's a hidden stairway behind this door." He tapped on the location. "Whoever occupies that office knows the staircase exists. It would be the perfect cover for people entering this building." He slid his finger over the Bureau of Truth building, his finger moving down to the basement, through a short tunnel, and back up the hidden staircase. "It's the perfect concealed route."

I sat back. "So, if we find out who has an office in there, we might find one of the twelve?"

"I would think so," Darby answered.

"Where's Claire's office?"

Darby brought both his hands up and redirected the hologram with a few swiping motions. The map shifted quickly, changing locations under his ministrations. He was getting good at running the program, which was a surprise to exactly no one. "I'm pretty sure this is her office." He tapped the screen, marking it with three red dots. "At least, this is where the orphan project is set up."

"Can you shrink it down so we can see everything at once?" I asked. He did, and I leaned forward, squinting. "They're not too far apart. She might have dealings there." I stood up, still feeling anxious. My friends' near-fatal dronecraft accident wasn't far from my mind. How could it be? "Where are they? I'm giving them ten minutes, and then we go after them."

"I'd wait," Darby cautioned. "Lockland and Claire interact all the time. They have a system in place. The medi-pod had to have taken a couple hours to finish the healing process on both Lockland and Bender."

"Yes, but it's been four hours, not two. Are you forgetting that the last time our friends didn't show up, they'd most likely be dead if we hadn't gone after them?" I asked.

"I haven't forgotten. But you went after them because they had a prisoner and a set time they were supposed to arrive back," Darby said. "We don't know where they are right now, so even if you wanted to, how would you find them?"

"They have to contact Claire by tech phone," I said. "I could use mine if I had to."

"True, but—"

A muffled sound cut him off.

"I'll check it out." Case stood, making his way back to the battery room, where he'd left the hatch ajar.

I followed. As soon as I got inside the room, I heard a woman's voice outside, and she sounded pissed. "That has to be Claire," I muttered, letting myself relax by a few degrees.

"I'm thinking the same thing," Case said.

A few minutes later, we heard Bender's voice. "We had no choice but to walk. We can't leave a craft out in the open when people are trying to track us down."

"Well, you could've dropped me off," Claire grumbled.

"I live and work in Government Square. What part of me is ready to hike through the wild for two kilometers?"

I climbed up, opening the hatch fully and popping my head out. "You're here," I said, catching sight of them, relieved to see Lockland walking without a limp.

"Of course we are," Claire answered with a wry grin. "Lockland beeped me and said it was important, so I came. It took me a while to lose my tail, but I did. Those bastards are still monitoring us."

I backed out of the way so they had enough room to enter.

Case helped Claire down, then Lockland and Bender jumped through. Case climbed up after, pulled the hatch closed, and secured it.

Bender proceeded to shake himself off like I imagined some kind of wild animal would have a long time ago. "Damn rain never stops," he growled as water droplets sprayed everywhere.

"Yeah," I quipped. "Thanks for sharing a portion of yours." I led them through the battery room.

As we passed, Claire exclaimed, "Are these batteries real?"

"Yep," I said. "Pretend you don't see them."

"Pretending," she said.

It was extremely illegal to have this much battery power. If we were caught, there would be severe consequences. "We're technically outside the city limits," I said. "So we'd have a solid argument for not revealing them."

"The jurisdiction of our government presides over everything within its reach," Claire stated, using her official government tone. "This is definitely within its reach. Not to mention, it looks like original government property." Her head bobbed as she examined the space, taking it all in.

I stopped next to a crate of dried protein flakes. "It is. Just keep pretending."

She smiled, spreading her arms wide, coming in for an embrace. I closed my eyes, relishing the fact that she was here, safe and sound. When she stepped away, she tugged off her helmet. Claire was strong and compact. Her creamy brown skin was flawless, her hair—even though it'd been tucked away under her helmet—was still perfectly secured in its tidy bun. "You know my pretending skills are worthless," she commented. "She who speaks the truth never lies. But I'll keep it to myself, like everything else. I won't have to lie if nobody asks me about it. And who's going to ask me if I know about secret barracks thirty kilometers south by the sea with a room full of batteries and enough food to feed a substantial number of people for years?"

I chuckled. "I hope nobody." Darby and Daze stood over by the seating area, waiting for us, the hologram map behind them. I led Claire over. "You remember Daze." I nodded toward the kid as Darby came around the couch to give Claire a hug.

"Of course," Claire said after she stepped back from Darby. "How are you, Daze? Is Holly treating you well? If she's not, I know some of her hidden weaknesses." She gave him a conspiratorial wink.

Daze surprised me by coming forward and wrapping his arms around Claire's waist. She rolled with it like a pro, hugging him back, leaning over to plant a kiss on the top of his head like they'd known each other forever.

But, honestly, the pair of them each had that effect on people, so it wasn't surprising. If he hadn't done it, and she hadn't reacted the way she had, I'd probably be more shocked.

"Holly is taking real good care of me," Daze said. "And look what we have, thanks to Lockland." He pulled Maisie out of his pocket.

Maisie took it from there, her shell lighting up as she flicked her colored lights around the room and intoned, "One unknown female detected. Vitals acceptable. Heart rate increased. One weapon, a half-tase, found."

Claire bent over, her face masked with wonder. "I'm Claire," she told the egg with complete assuredness. "Glad to hear my vitals are acceptable. I have a few more weapons at my residence, but if you know how to work a half-tase, it can be just as lethal as a full. Don't rule me out of the game just yet."

"Of which game are you speaking, Claire?" Maisie asked. It was the first time I'd heard the status reader ask a question, which sounded strange.

"Why, the game of life, of course." Claire chuckled as she straightened. "This thing can't be too smart if it can't catch my play on words."

"Puns and sarcasm are difficult for me to discern," Maisie responded. "However, my program, once triggered by this play on words, will remember it. So don't rule me out of the game just yet."

Claire's eyebrows rose to her hairline, and I laughed. "I stand corrected," she told the egg. "I won't rule you out."

"Thank you," Maisie said. "It is nice to make your acquaintance."

"Honestly," I said, still chuckling, "she'll pick up on anything if you give her enough time. It's actually freaky how much she can infer from a benign conversation." I made my way around the seating area and sat. "I want to show you this. Darby thinks he found a substantial lead. I know you guys just arrived, but we should talk about this and get organized." Claire took a seat next to me. "The last time we talked was at the Emporium," I said to her. "You indicated that things were happening and that certain people were trying to sway attitudes and loyalties. You said you'd found out about this secret group, the Bureau of Truth, for the first time. Fill us in on what's happened since then."

Bender grabbed a chair and slid it over, straddling it backward. I was happy to see a fully healed Lockland sit next to Darby, taking in the map with a curious expression. Case sat on my other side, and Daze knelt by the table, settling Maisie on the glass top directly beneath the hologram.

"A lot has happened in a short amount of time,"

Claire started. "Murmurs have turned into whispers, and whispers are becoming loud. I still haven't been able to find anything substantial on the Bureau of Truth—other than it's been rumored to have been making Plush all this time and feeding it to those poor addicted souls. As I was telling Lockland and Bender on the way over, the government is like a frayed cloth beginning to tear. My network of loyalists is willing to defend the government as is, for better or worse, but fear is affecting most everyone. It's clear that a substantial number are beginning to support a revolution." She shook her head. "I don't understand it. People who choose to serve do it because they have a passion for helping others. They would feel lost without working toward bettering lives in this cruel world. It must come from the heart"—she placed a hand over her chest—"as we get no compensation, other than a decent place to live, in exchange for our service. We do our jobs because we have hope that if we help, we can make this world incrementally better each and every day. A revolution would mean war. People would die needlessly. Then who knows who would gain power? People are making these decisions not based on fact, but on speculation and gossip, which is insane."

I thought about what she was saying. "You don't receive a wage now, but that wasn't how things began, right?" I asked. "When coin was still traded, and before The Water Initiative left, government workers were paid a nominal wage, and the government collected taxes, mostly in the form of salvaged items, but it collected them all the same. For the first thirty years after the meteor struck, the government tried to hold the world together, providing for the people, keeping the structure similar to the way it was before disaster struck."

"Yes, that's true," Claire said. "But it hasn't been like that for so many years, many have forgotten."

"What if I told you at least twelve haven't forgotten?" I said. "And those twelve might've struck a deal with The Water Initiative before they left. The bureau might've been formed just before the initiative to cull the so-called defective residents of the city and remake those remaining into an obedient populace. These people would then wait for the Flotilla to come back. And once the water dwellers arrived on land, the groups would combine their resources to create a viable city, reinstating currency and kickstarting a new era of industry."

Claire sat back, crossing her legs. "If I'd heard that same story a few weeks ago, I would've said you were out of your mind. But now, in light of the new information coming out, I would believe that—as farfetched as it sounds. Most everyone in the government believes the Flotilla didn't succeed, that the ships went down and all was lost. They took communication devices with them, but we've never heard a word, as far as I know. It's been more than thirty years."

"I'm sure Bender and Lockland filled you in about

what we learned from Reed," I said. "The Bureau of Truth has their own communication setup. Bandwidths we knew nothing about. It could be that the Flotilla has been communicating with them in secret. The bureau has been very patient, waiting for the perfect time to enact their strategy. They've been building an army down South, readying the city, and it all points to this building right here." I touched my finger on the hologram in front of us. "There's a medi-pod in the basement that has the potential to cure seekers, and in the building next door, Darby found a hidden stairwell that leads to this tunnel." I ran my finger along the route. "That would explain how the twelve are moving around without being seen entering this building." I used both my hands to shift the hologram so it was in front of Claire. My technique was a little choppy, but not bad for my first try. "We need to figure out whose office is right here. This is where the stairwell access is." I made small circular movements with my finger. "Darby thinks this used to be the housing building."

"It was." Claire nodded, scooting forward on the couch. "I've been there many times. It's used now for general assembly talks and private group meetings." She examined the hologram. She was quiet for a few moments, her expression darkening.

"Do you know who works in that office?" I prodded.

"Are you sure this is the right place?" Claire asked.

"Fairly certain. The stairway behind the door is a dead giveaway." I trailed my finger, once again, through the room and down the stairs. "It leads to this tunnel, which leads to this room in the building next door. It's the perfect cover to slip away without being seen."

"Then from that room," Darby said, taking over, "there are two different ways to access the inside of this building. Right here, up these internal stairs. Or the door here on the same level." He tapped the image. "We're trying to get to a medi-pod we think is there, which is highlighted on Roman's map, but not on this one. This feed was taken right before the meteor struck. Everything matches up, so it has to be the right building."

By the look on Claire's face, she knew who occupied the office in the building next door. "Who is it, Claire?"

"It's Albert." Her eyes traced away from the map as she brought a hand up to her throat and murmured softly, "How can it be Albert?"

Chapter 22

"Who's Albert?" I asked.

Claire stood abruptly, moving away from the seating area. I followed. A few steps later, she spun around, anger brimming on her features. "He's a friend, that's who," she said. "He also happens to be a loyalist. He's in our group. The man has been a member of the loyalist group for years."

I considered the implications.

The Bureau of Truth was cagey, that was for certain. Not only were they trying to blend in, but they'd affiliated themselves with the opposition, managing to fool people like Claire into believing they were the kind of people who were against revolution, when they were the ones kindling it.

"Have you shared anything about us with him?" I paced to a pillar and leaned against it. "Has he asked you probing questions?"

"Yes, he's asked," she said. "But they're always

framed under the guise of inquiring about my personal life." She waved a hand in the air. "But you needn't worry. I haven't been foolish enough to answer any of his questions, or anyone else's, for that matter. I keep my private life concealed, as I always have. In fact, recently I've gone to great lengths to disavow your group and its violence." My expression reflected my surprise. "I had no choice." She turned and paced. "Your defeat of that group from down South has been openly discussed. It was the only thing I could think of to throw off the scent of our union. I believe I've been convincing, but I guess we won't know for sure until this all plays out."

I pushed off the pillar and walked back over to the seating unit and took a seat. "If members of the Bureau of Truth are masquerading as loyalists, then they've handed us an advantage." I met Claire's gaze. "We need to get you back before it arouses more suspicion. And then we need you to set up a meeting with the loyalists. Can you arrange it for tomorrow?"

"Likely," she answered. "I can pretend I have new information to share. They know I have sources, but not who."

"You will have new information. Vital information," I said, glancing at Lockland across the tech table. "About the movements of our group."

Lockland nodded. "False information." He leaned forward, examining the hologram. "Then, when we know the majority will go to place X, we'll be at place Y."

"If place Y equals this building"—I tapped the map—"you're exactly right. But we'll only get one chance. Doing it this way will expose Claire. But it won't matter if we achieve full takeover." Full takeover equaled eliminating the threat completely.

"But we have to keep this from the rest of the government," Darby said. "If people notice twelve government workers disappearing abruptly, it will get back to the militia quickly."

"I agree. We do it stealthily," I said. "The objective is for Tillman to keep thinking everything is going smoothly up here. We enter the building while they're trying to track us down, following Claire's lead, and wait for the rest to return. We take them out, but we do it quietly."

"And we make it look like Reed has succeeded in his mission, and we're no longer a threat," Lockland said. "We can do that by recording Reed saying something of the sort and playing it over their private bandwidth once we have access to the building. They'll figure it out eventually, but this should give us time to launch an attack of our own down South."

I nodded. Phase two of this plan would be more complicated, but taking out the Bureau of Truth here was the starting place. Not to mention, we needed access to the medi-pod, if it was operational. Ned and Mary were holed up, waiting for our help.

"I like it," Bender said. "At this point, we don't have a whole hell of a lot of choice. They're closing in. There's no doubt they're waiting right now for one of us to come home. Their UACs have to be darting all over the city. I bet they're pissed off they can't locate us. If we strike before they know we're back, it could work."

Case chimed in, "It's risky, since we don't know if we can make it through this tunnel here." He tapped the screen by our underground hidey-hole, highlighting the area, which looked perfectly clear and undamaged in the hologram, but wouldn't look anything like that in real life. "But every scenario I've gone over in my mind is full of risk. Our best chance is to go in when they're not expecting it."

"We're outnumbered," Lockland said. "But since we've gathered intel on them from Reed, we know they're spread out over great distances, so there's a higher likelihood we can achieve success if we treat each area as its own zone. For now, the important part is keeping Tillman away. If he brings his troops to the city, this could be over before it starts. From the tech you two spotted down South alone"—he glanced between Case and me—"they have access to a hell of a lot more resources than we do."

"Once we secure the building," I said, "we essentially take over their operations. Maybe we keep one of them alive and give them Babble." I turned to Claire, who was walking toward the tech table. "Once we gain the upper hand, you'll know exactly who they are. How long do you think your loyalists group can cover for them at work? You'll need to make excuses for why they haven't shown up."

"Realistically," she answered, "three or four days at the most. There's only a few hundred of us in the entirety of the government, so gossip will begin immediately." She sat next to me. "You all believe there are twelve key figures leading this anarchy, but I know for a fact that those twelve have convinced others to join their cause. They've been careful to prey on the disgruntled and hopeless—those who have the most to lose—and it's worked. Albert is older, in his early fifties, but I would bet not all the members are that old. In order to keep something like this active for thirty years, they have to have been recruiting new people into their fold. It angers me that this has been happening right under my nose all this time and I never knew."

"Don't feel bad," I reassured her. "They didn't go near you, other than Albert asking you a few questions, because they know where you stand ethically and morally. If they had, their cover would've been blown a long time ago. Just like you said, they target the weak and disgruntled. They've been sneaky and careful, and it's worked for them. That also means their casual, or new, supporters likely have less of a backbone, which bodes well for us." I smiled. "Do you think the loyalists can round up the bureau's supporters? You'll most likely have to use force once you figure out who they are." Claire didn't participate in combat. Her greatest asset to the group was working from the inside.

Slowly, she nodded. "Once the twelve are gone,

there will be gossip, and I'd like to think some panic and erratic behavior from those who think they might be next. The loyalist group is over forty members strong, so even if all twelve members of the Bureau of Truth are within the group—which I don't believe they are—we should have enough strength to keep their supporters locked down, for a while at least."

"When the deed is done, which will take time, since some members will be on-site and some will be gone, we'll help you contain the supporters," Lockland said. "With our access to Babble, we'll be able to surmise the intent of each one and how far their convictions go in favor of the revolution. Your group can work on convincing them that continuing to support the opposition is a bad idea, and for some, that will be enough."

"For others..." Claire's voice trailed off.

She was a lover of life, which was why she'd dedicated her life to helping people. War and uprising were never easy, and yes, people would lose their lives.

I grasped her hand. "I know this is hard, but there's also incredibly good news to go with all the crappy stuff. What lies in the basement of that building has the potential to help thousands of people. Remember when you said most of the government would rally around a cure for the seekers? It could be right here." I gestured at the hologram. "That will be our rallying point for the remaining government body. Focus on that, and not the other stuff, if you can. And there's even more good news coming. I'm not sure how much

Lockland and Bender told you about what we found down South, but we discovered scientists who've been working on solving problems for the betterment of humanity for as long as the Bureau of Truth has been trying to undermine it—if not longer. They have inoculations, cures for disease, resources, and they're growing plants. They have seeds and bio-printed food that tastes like nothing you've ever imagined." I gave her hand a squeeze. "Claire, this will be the start of a new world, one you've been working toward your entire life. But if the Bureau of Truth gets there first, a group of vicious militants will rob most of humanity of that dream. So we have to do everything in our power to fight for the majority, and once we succeed, we can be a part of reshaping the city into a better place." I hadn't felt this much hope in a long time—if ever.

I wasn't alone.

Bender stood abruptly, his chair clattering forward. "Let's figure out the story Claire tells her group tomorrow, then I'm taking her back. Alone. I've got a way in that will be undetectable. It'll get her close enough to her residence so she gets back safely. The more time this takes, the more risk involved. They were following her, but they don't know where she went."

"Done," I said. "After that, we perfect our plan and get some sleep. We enter the city tomorrow at blackout."

Chapter 23

"Are you sure this is right?" Darby asked.

"*Shh,*" I said.

"Why are you shushing me?" Darby rotated his head to look around. "There's no one else here."

"Voices carry in a tunnel," I replied. "They could have sensors or amplifiers set up. We have no idea what kind of traps are waiting for us." Darby and I stood outside our underground safe house in the hypertube chamber, a small space where the airlock used to be.

Lockland, Bender, and Case were inside the mag-lev train, readying the weaponry. Lockland had made it to one of his stashes before arriving here and had managed to bring a barrel laser big enough to sear a hole through rock. That would make it easier to deal with any walls we encountered. He'd strapped it to his back and wore a cloak, much like Cozzi would have back in the day. Poor Cozzi. I wished he were here to see all the progress the world was set to make.

None of us had gone anywhere near our residences. We'd entered the city hours ago under the cover of blackout, leaving our crafts a few kilometers outside the east entrance, slipping in one by one, disappearing in different directions. We'd met up here less than thirty minutes ago.

"I doubt they have any amplifiers set in this direction," Darby said.

"They could," I countered. Although, since the Bureau of Truth had gone unchallenged for thirty years, there was a good chance they'd gotten complacent over the years.

"I'm pretty sure we're going to find the tunnel impassable." Darby gestured in the direction we were set to go in a few moments. "These air pockets, like the one we're in now, are a rarity in this city." They were indeed. It'd taken us years to find them. "The damage done underground by the meteor and the ensuing sea-level rise was cataclysmic."

"Yeah, I know," I said. "I'm familiar with the topography of the city. I'm sure we'll encounter some issues, but with that barrel laser, we have a good chance of getting through even if it's blocked."

"The laser blasts are going to make a lot of noise with all the falling rocks and debris," Darby said.

I turned to study my friend. "Are you always such a pessimist? Or is this the first time I'm actually noticing it?"

Darby kicked a rock, and it skittered a few meters before hitting a large chunk of concrete, bouncing off.

"I'm not a pessimist. I'm just not normally involved in combat." Darby had my HydroSol gun. It looked odd tucked into his waistband.

"I know you're nervous," I said, my tone changing. "But we need everyone for this. We only get one chance." I held up a single finger. "And if all goes according to our stellar plan, you're just here for backup."

He nodded. "I know." He shuffled his feet again.

"You did a great job at the Emporium when you came to my rescue when Hutch injected me with Plush," I told him, trying to cheer him up.

"I didn't have to fire my weapon," he said. "You guys had it all figured out by the time I arrived."

"Well, there's always the medi-pod. If it hasn't been destroyed, it will be awesome to see it in all its glory."

"It's probably not there," he said.

"Okay"—I spread my arms out—"I'm trying here. If I am, you have to, too. It's only fair. If you remember correctly, I voted for you to stay at the barracks with Daze." The only thing in the entire plan that I hadn't agreed with was leaving Daze alone to guard Reed. We'd given Reed another dose of Babble, and after the interrogation, we'd tranqed him, leaving Daze with enough doses to keep the guy knocked out for a while. But I still didn't like it.

Daze had argued that he was strong enough to do the job, and everyone else had agreed with him. It wasn't that I didn't think he was strong enough—but the kid had a heart, and from what we'd seen in the short time we'd known the guy, Reed was manipulative.

I'd reluctantly given in to the majority, but only after Daze promised to keep Reed out cold the entire time. The kid had sworn he would, and there was nothing else to do but hope everything went according to plan.

"I'll stop being a downer," Darby started, "but only if you promise me we're getting out of this alive."

"Nobody's dying." I kicked a rock of my own. "Well, except the bad guys." I reached into my pocket and pulled out my timepiece. It read six thirty a.m. I shook my head. "We have to get started soon," I said. "We can't miss the nine a.m. deadline." The story we'd come up with for Claire to tell the loyalists was that we'd be entering the city in The North this morning, rather than at blackout like they'd be expecting. If the Bureau of Truth was smart, they'd have already sent people to that location to wait. But even if they hadn't, the bureau's headquarters should be pared down to just a few by nine.

At that moment, Lockland, Bender, and Case exited the train. Lockland nodded. "Let's go."

We began our trek through the tunnel, stopping short at a pile of impassable rock twenty meters in. Lockland got his barrel laser out, and we began the task of burning our way through.

After a few hours of work, I pulled my timepiece out again. "We're going to have to work faster, or we're going to risk more people being at home, which makes everything more complicated."

"We're going as fast as we can." Bender wiped his brow with a forearm. "Some of these chunks weigh a hundred kilos apiece. It takes time to move them." Bender and Case had been doing the heavy lifting, while Lockland operated the barrel laser. Then Darby and I came in and cleaned out the small stuff.

It was grueling, slow work all around. I shot Darby a look. "Don't even say it."

"I'm not saying anything," Darby responded blandly. "Except that, by my calculations, we have more than forty meters to go before we reach the edge of the building. Although the barrel-laser fallout is not as loud as expected, we risk a lot by using it the closer we get."

"We can decide that when we get there," I said. "As of right now, we don't know if the tunnel is going to be blocked the entire way. Maisie hasn't been able to give us an accurate reading, but I refuse to join the pessimist camp." The status reader was having trouble gauging how extensive the debris pile was. Her sensors were picking up rock and concrete everywhere, along with steel and rebar, which made it hard for her to pinpoint what we specifically wanted to know.

Case had his shoulder propped against the tunnel, taking a break. We all stood in a small space no more than three meters wide and just tall enough for Bender not to scrape his head on the rough, rocky ceiling. "We should expect company," Case said. "If I were running the Bureau of Truth, I would send most people to the rendezvous, but keep a few back to monitor the situation."

I took a seat on a large chunk of concrete that had just been relocated. "I would, too," I said. "Maisie can give us an accurate reading when we arrive. Claire's story was purposely vague to require manpower on their part or risk losing us upon entry into the city. She told them she wasn't sure which of two entrances we'd come through, and they're four kilometers apart."

Case nodded. "Darby's right about the noise. If there are a few people left in that building, they could pick up on the vibrations." As the rocks came down, they shook the ground.

"We don't have another choice," I replied. "Plus, we don't know how far this current blockage reaches. We could be free of it in less than ten meters." I stood, clapping my hands on my pants, concrete dust puffing everywhere. There was one good thing about being in the tunnel—no rain. "Come on, let's keep going."

Lockland was one step ahead of me, aiming the barrel laser and firing as he swung it back and forth. Another rush of debris clattered to the ground, rock and concrete that had been cut from the blockage with the high-powered, super-hot laser.

Once Lockland stepped back, the four of us went in and picked up the remnants, moving as much as we could as quickly as possible. "Zap this one again," Bender ordered, gesturing at a large, intact piece of concrete. "It's too big to haul out."

Lockland obliged, and Case and Bender went in to pick up the smaller pieces.

"Hey, look through there." I pointed toward the

hole that had been created once Bender and Case had moved the debris. "It's black, not gray." I withdrew Maisie from my vest.

Darby came to stand next to me. "I think you're right. That might be clear tunnel behind there."

"Maisie, do you detect any solid rock blocking our way more than three meters in front of us?" I asked.

Her lights darted around. "I detect concrete, iron, steel, clay—"

"Yes, I know," I said. "But is there a large pocket of air in front of us?"

"I detect a large amount of oxygen and hydrogen directly in front of you," she answered.

"I'm taking that as a yes." I thumped the back of my hand against Darby's upper arm, pointing. "See? I was right. You are wrong. Pessimists never win."

"Ow." He rubbed his shoulder. "This has nothing to do with being an optimist or a pessimist and everything to do with how this city was damaged nearly sixty years ago. There are bound to be pockets, but as I said before, they are few and far between."

Case began to heave some large pieces away from the front of the hole. I bent down to help him. We dragged a large rock backward a few meters. With a little help from Lockland, we cleared the space enough for us to get through. Bender tossed an ultra-light into the void.

The tunnel lit up in front of us.

I dropped to my knees and crawled through. On the other side, I stood, brushing myself off as I waited for the others. They came through one by one. "I don't see any major damage ahead." I gestured at some large bouldery-looking objects. "Other than a few hunks of ceiling that have come down, but we can maneuver around those, no problem." These tunnels had been built with two-meter-thick steel bracing, so it was unsurprising that some of it had stayed standing after the onslaught. "There's a curve up ahead. We won't know if it'll stay clear until we get farther."

We began to jog.

Less than twenty meters in, we came to another standstill. But this time it wasn't a natural cave-in. It was manmade. I placed my palm against the rock structure—a wall that had been assembled to keep people out. It didn't feel that strong. I gave it a tentative push. There was a little movement, but not much.

"Be careful," Darby said. "If you knock something loose, it could cause a landslide situation."

I took a step back, placing my hands on my hips. Without fishing Maisie out of my pocket, I asked, "Maisie, can you tell me the thickness of the wall one meter in front of me?"

She responded, albeit muffled, "Solid material detected. Approximately one-point-two meters thick."

"We have no idea who erected this, the Bureau of Truth or someone else," I said. "But if it had been me, I would've wired it somehow."

Lockland stood next to me, the barrel laser strapped to his back. He put his hands out, doing the same thing I'd just done, testing it as he walked the width of the tunnel. "We have to assume it was put here by the Bureau of Truth to keep any inquiring minds from coming from this way. We also have to assume there are alarms or hydro-bombs on the other side set to activate if this wall fails."

"If we can't topple this," I said, "we have to go back now and try to find a new route." Which would be difficult, because we'd have to enter through the front of the building, which would draw attention.

"I didn't say we can't get through," Lockland said. "We just have to make sure it doesn't come down, which will take some finesse on our part."

Darby moved to one end, tapping on some of the stones. "If we have something to brace a small section, it might work."

"There were some pieces of steel in the tunnel," Case said, turning to go back the way we'd just come. "I'll grab them."

The rest of us began to inspect the structure, looking for the best way to get through that wouldn't bring the whole damn thing down.

"What about right here?" Bender gestured to a portion of the wall that consisted of smaller rocks surrounded by bigger ones. "The key will be supporting it as we take rocks out, which will be hard, but not impossible. But this area is big enough for us to get through."

"Looks as good as any," Lockland said.

Behind us, Case came through the hole, dragging two long steel girders behind him.

Darby inspected them. "Those will work, but they need to be shorter."

Case nodded toward me. "You can cut through them with your Gem, if your hand is steady enough."

Bender snorted as I countered, "Is that a challenge?" I withdrew my laser.

"Not a chance," Case answered, a grin quirking up one side of his mouth.

"Before you cut them," Darby said, "let's make sure we get them roughly the right size. The first few need to be angled, but they don't have to be very thick. The wall isn't that wide."

"Point to where you want it, and I'll make the cuts," I said.

Darby did some rough sizing with his hands stretched over the area of wall. Then he bent over the girders. "Right here." He made a slashing movement with his wrist. "And right here. Make sure they're at an angle, like I indicated."

"Got it." I knew the timing of my Gem perfectly, so it wouldn't be an issue, but just to be sure, I ordered, "Everybody, back up."

"Please don't tell me Case is right," Bender grunted, "and your aim is terrible. This isn't the way I want to go out."

"Nobody's dying," I said. "Just get back in *case* I hit something reflective." The steel was old and rusty, so it shouldn't be a problem. But you never knew.

"Hilarious," Darby said. "Now make the cuts."

"Always the taskmaster." I made the first slice,

timing my tug on the trigger just right, giving it a three-second burst and flicking my wrist. Then I did the next one.

Darby rushed forward, careful not to touch the end I'd just seared. Once it was cool enough, he turned the girder on its side. "Now cut the entire thing down the length of the middle."

"Prop it up against the tunnel wall." I gestured to the area that would work. Darby arranged it, and I started to make the cut, which would take at least five seconds running cleanly down the middle, but after three, my Gem sputtered out. "Damn." I glanced down at my weapon, hoping it was just out of fuel and not dead, as I dug around in my pocket for more nano-carbon cubes.

"What the hell?" Bender said. "It's a good thing you found out you were out of power now, rather than once we get inside." His tone indicated my negligence could've cost someone their life, and he was right. That would've been in the unforgivable-mistake category.

"It's not like you to run out of fuel," Lockland said.

I shot a furtive glance in Case's direction, then put my head down, placing the cartridges inside. "I usually do it every other morning, but the other day I was a little distracted."

"Distracted how?" Darby asked.

"None of your business," I muttered, lifting my now fully powered gun and aiming it at the girder. My actions drowned out any further inquiry. The metal promptly fell in two pieces. Then I hit the next one. When it was done, I asked, "Are we finished?"

"Yes," Darby said, dragging one of them in front of the wall. Bender and Lockland picked up the other three and brought them over. "We're going to start right here." Darby gestured to a large rock a meter and a half off the ground. "Case, take that stone out, and then we'll brace the opening."

We followed Darby's orders until the gap in front of us was big enough to squeeze through. The only problem was, the girders were in the way. The wall had undulated a bit as we worked, but not as much as I'd thought it would. We all took a step back to inspect the hole.

"We're going to have to take some of the steel out in order to get through," Lockland said.

I reached for my timepiece, a throwback from a hundred years ago. It was a good thing we'd been able to repurpose some old technology. Not being able to coordinate time would be a serious hardship. According to the clock, we'd been at all this for a half hour. "Once we're on the other side, we have less than an hour to get to the building."

"Okay, let's take out the lower brace," Darby said. "It should still hold. But we're going to have to go through fast."

I nodded. "Get your chromes on. You're going to be the one scanning for bombs and other traps as we move." Bender had already thrown his ultra-light through the new hole. Nothing seemed amiss from this side, but traps were called traps for a reason. "I'll go first."

Lockland edged me out of the way. "No, I'm going first. I have to see if this barrel laser fits through the opening. If not, we have to remove more rocks." Lockland got on his knees, managing to sneak through the opening, but just barely.

I followed, then Bender, Darby, and Case.

Nothing had exploded, so things were looking good.

"I don't see anything out of the ordinary," Darby said as he stood, clicking through the dials on his chromoscopes. "There's not even any bio-residue, which means no one's been in this area for a while."

"I didn't even know you could pick up bio-residue with those glasses," I said. "I just look for the obvious stuff."

"You have to know where to look on the gamma setting," Darby said. "Fresh skin gives off small amounts of light. So does sweat."

"Good to know. Though, sweat wouldn't be a big indicator unless somebody decided to swipe their armpit along the wall."

Bender chuckled. "My head sweats. So do my hands."

"My back sweats," Darby complained. "So, for example, if I leaned against this wall, it would leave an imprint." He made a move to demonstrate, but I grabbed him by the arm and tugged him along.

"Okay, okay." I laughed. "I get it. But even so, sweat evaporates quickly."

"Yeah," Darby said. "But the leftover molecules can be seen for up to twenty-four hours. But they're super faint."

"Let's have Maisie do a cursory check." I pulled the status reader out of my vest. "Maisie, scan for hydrogen bombs, weapons, and human activity. Exclude us from your scan."

A moment later, she replied, "No hydrogen weapons in the vicinity. I detect more than one hundred humans within a five-kilometer radius. All of them are a minimum of five meters above you."

"Thank you, Maisie. Keep on high alert. We will be approaching our destination shortly."

"I will keep my scanners engaged," she agreed.

We followed Lockland. In less than ten meters, his hand went up. His head shifted to the right, then the left, as he scanned the area. We were at another curve in the tunnel. It was impossible to know if the tunnel was blocked farther to the left or not, because it was beyond our field of view.

Lockland began to move toward something.

He was almost in front of it before I saw it was a door. It was old and dirty with age, nearly black with grime.

We'd made it. And we were early.

Chapter 24

"Stand back. This might blow," Lockland commanded as he pulled a weighted hook out of his pocket. Once we were all back, he expertly tossed it onto the handle of the door. It caught the edge, forcing the lever down.

The door didn't blow, but it stayed latched.

"It's locked," Bender said.

"Yeah," Lockland said, moving forward to retrieve the hook. "Not surprising. But we didn't know if the handle was rigged. Now we know."

I said, "Maisie told us she didn't detect any hydrogen behind it."

"Hydrogen isn't the only way to trigger an explosion," Lockland replied.

"That's true," I said. "And Maisie's not infallible." For us to put our unfettered trust in the egg would be silly. Maisie hadn't made a mistake yet, but she certainly could. Her database was at least sixty years old. Eventually, she would come across something she didn't understand.

Darby and Case wandered down the tunnel a little farther, inspecting the area around the door.

"According to the hologram map," Darby called, "this entire expanse leads into the smaller tunnel that connects to the Bureau of Truth building. It was a branch off of the main zoom tunnels, meant specifically for commuters who worked in these buildings. I'm thinking we shouldn't enter through any door, just because we could encounter something unexpected. But we can enter anywhere along here." He gestured in front of him.

I said, somewhat skeptically, "You want us to blast our way through now? Right when we're outside the building? You told us noise would put us at risk." I gestured upward to where I thought the building would be located. "We're too close."

Darby quirked a brow at me. "The barrel laser itself isn't loud. It's the unstable debris crashing down, like I told you before. If Lockland shoots a clean line through here"—he patted the relatively smooth wall—"it will produce a hole, but the wall won't come down around it, because it's not made of rubble. It's solid concrete. He'll have to do it a few times to make the gap wide enough for us to get through, but the rest of the wall should hold. These walls were constructed out of concrete forms reinforced by steel. They're sturdy, which is why they're still standing."

"Sounds good to me," Bender said.

Lockland unstrapped the laser from his back, maneuvering so he was in front of where Darby had indicated. "Are you sure this is the right spot?" Lockland asked.

"I did a rough calculation, and we should be about four meters from the interior door, according to my memory. If you hit something through the tunnel on the other side, it shouldn't do any damage to the building," Darby answered. "It's ten to fifteen meters farther to the left once we're inside."

"Move back," Lockland instructed. "The area inside might be rigged."

"If you hit a bomb with your laser, we're all done for, no matter where we stand," Bender grumbled, but moved back anyway.

Lockland grunted as he positioned the laser, locked between his arms and braced against his abdomen. "That all depends on how big the bomb is." He shot a clean line through the wall, then slid half a meter to the right and did it again. The third blast was aimed at the bottom, centered between the other two.

When he was done, there was a clean triangle big enough for us to fit through.

We all waited, listening.

The rest of us had drawn our weapons, including Darby. After a full minute, Lockland poked his head through to take a look.

"What do you see?" I asked, coming up behind him.

He pulled back, staying on his haunches. "Nothing. It's dark. We need another ultra-light."

Bender's light was working for us in here, so I drew mine out, flicked it on, and tossed it inside. Lockland put his head back through. "It smells dank and musty," he said. "This tunnel has been sealed up for a while."

"Have Maisie do another scan," Darby said, "while I check it out with my chromes." Lockland nodded and stepped back as Darby took his place.

The status reader was in my palm. "Maisie, check for any traps and human activity," I said. "I want to know specifically if there are any humans, other than us, within a twenty-meter radius."

"I detect no hydrogen or frequency units nearby. I detect four humans within twenty meters."

"Are they above us?" I asked.

"Yes," she replied.

"So, maybe four stayed behind?" I tucked the status reader back in my pocket. "We won't know until we're closer and Maisie can give us a more specific distance."

Darby did a visual scan. After he gave us the okay, we all climbed through the opening, entering a narrow hallway. We were all extremely cognizant that there could be surprises waiting for us along the way. But judging by the musty smell, Lockland was right that this space had been entombed for a long time, which likely meant that even if there were traps, nobody had maintained them for a while.

The area was more like a corridor than a tunnel.

In less than twenty paces, we saw a door that most likely led between the two buildings. This was where commuters would've entered to head to work, back when these structures were office buildings of some kind. Once inside, there would be a door to the right, leading into the basement of the bureau headquarters, where the medi-pod should be located. To the left would be a door that led to a short tunnel and the secret staircase in the old housing building. All according to the hologram map anyway. Then, from the medi-pod room, there were two other doors that accessed the interior of the bureau building.

We gathered around the entry point.

Lockland pressed his back against the wall next to the door, the barrel laser under one arm. "Once we breach this, there's no going back."

I nodded. "If we can avoid setting off any alarms on the way in, we'll certainly get farther without interference."

"Once inside the medi-pod room," Bender said, "Lockland and I go left. Holly, Case, and Darby go up the stairs. I'll rig the door we go through with a hydro-bomb, so anybody coming in behind us gets blasted."

"Sounds good," I said, holding Maisie up a few centimeters in front of the door. "Maisie, do a scan. We're looking for anything that might harm us. We're also looking for any humans in extremely close proximity, anywhere from a few meters away to a few stories directly above our heads."

"I detect no explosives in any form. One titanium bolt detected one-meter east. There are two humans, one located seven meters above you and one located eighteen-point-three meters above you."

"How thick is the titanium bolt?" I asked.

"Ten centimeters in diameter," she answered.

"That's a big-ass bolt," I said.

"It exceeds residential standards," she replied. "According to my database, these types of locking mechanisms were used in bank vaults."

My eyebrows shot up. "Should we risk lasering through something that big? Taking that thing out is bound to make some noise."

"Hand me the status reader," Darby said. I dropped Maisie into his hand, and he walked back down the corridor approximately three meters. "Maisie, scan for medical apparatuses, particularly a working medi-pod. Key features include diagnostic scopes in the form of glass magnifiers, molecule sensitivity components, magnetic laser interferometers, and critical reforming disks."

Maisie got to work.

"Damn," I muttered. "He's so much better about ordering her around than I am."

Case chuckled. "He should be. He speaks her language."

"He should be in charge of her from now on," I said as we waited for Maisie to formulate her response. But even if the medi-pod wasn't there, we were going in. This entire mission had become something so much larger than saving Mary and other seekers.

Maisie came back a moment later with, "Medi-pod detected."

I exhaled, refraining from joyous excitement until we saw the thing in one piece.

"Precise location required. Use distance measurements from this exact point, coupled with directional locators," Darby commanded. "Relay in meters rounded to one decimal."

It didn't take her long. "Medi-pod is located two-point-two meters to the south and nine-point-one meters east."

"Please supply interior north wall location from this position," Darby said. "Wall definition: Material used may be wood or metal, insulation unknown, but likely polymer fibers, not more than six centimeters thick."

"Wall detected to the north," Maisie said. "One-point-three meters from this position."

Darby turned to us. "Okay, according to Maisie, we have roughly a two-meter area to play with right around here." He indicated a meter to the right, extending his arms. "If we laser through here, we won't hit the medi-pod."

I hesitated. "I don't know about going through the wall. There could be tons of stuff in that room. It's probably a lab, like all the other locations. If we go through the door, at least we know there's nothing behind it. Or there shouldn't be."

"You might be right," Darby said, "but luckily we can ask." He lofted the egg up, even though it wasn't necessary. I'd done it, too. It was like we thought the status reader had actual eyeballs. "Maisie, identify objects no more than two meters in front of this location."

"Identifying shelving, glass vials, medical tools, implements—"

"Stop," I commanded. "It's definitely a lab. I say we go through the door. Unless someone has a better idea."

Darby asked Maisie, "Relay tactical entry to breach room in front of us with lowest percentage of being discovered." Darby shrugged his shoulders at our surprised expressions. "She's military grade. It's worth a try. Whoever programmed her would've included tactical scenarios for her to access."

"In order to perform request, I require a list of resources," she replied.

"Barrel laser, Gem laser, Blaster, HydroSol, Pulse, taser." Darby paused in clicking through our arsenal. "What weapon do you use again?" he asked Bender.

"I have a Web laser and a Pulse," he answered.

I glanced at Bender. "Since when do you carry a Pulse?"

"I've always had it." He shrugged. "I've only started carrying it around recently."

"Huh," I said. I guessed it made sense. *Recently* was when things had taken a turn in our lives. "Maisie, I have a few blades on me, not to mention Case has a hot-laser key, and I've a frequency key, among the supplies in my vest, including my magic cord."

Darby nodded. "Maisie, if necessary, scan each of us for compatibility needs."

Maisie's lights flickered on and off for at least a minute as she calculated an entry plan. I was beginning to wonder how we'd ever survived without her. Going in blind, versus going in with critical information, was no contest.

She finally said, "Entry through wall advisable. Barrel laser engaged. Calculated risk of detection: four percent. Human-hearing range and thickness of the walls prevent detection. For all other entry points, risk is elevated."

"State precise location of entry from fixed position," Darby said.

"One-point-six meters south, one-point-two meters up from ground level. Three blasts required."

Impressive. "I guess going through the wall it is," I said.

Chapter 25

"Did Maisie really just take us through cabinets?" I whispered as I crawled out of what used to be some sort of built-in storage unit.

Spotting what was sitting in the corner, I forgot my question almost immediately. The medi-pod was completely intact.

I made my way over and set a gloved hand, the one that wasn't holding my Gem at attention, on top of it and walked along the side, taking it all in.

Darby's hushed voice came from behind me. "You were right. They didn't destroy it."

I glanced at him. "I've never been so happy to be right about something in my entire life." My voice was extremely low. No one had come running, but there was still time. If this truly was the medi-pod that Roman had worked on, everything in our world had just shifted. Thousands of lives could be recovered. The stakes in winning this battle with the

Bureau of Truth were even higher now.

Case emerged from the hole, his gaze locked on the medi-pod. "It's here. That means we have to succeed."

"I was just thinking the same thing," I murmured. "A loss is unacceptable."

Lockland came next and immediately paced to the door on the left that led to the interior of the building, placing his head close, listening. Bender moved toward the door that faced the housing building, drawing a hydro-bomb out of his pocket, rigging it on the handle.

The other door that accessed the building was situated to my right and up a set of steep metal steps. Darby pulled Maisie out and whispered, "Engage reply at ten decibels. Locate humans within this building. Instead of distance measurements, use floor diagrams relating to internal database map."

I raised an eyebrow. "If she has a map of this building, it's over sixty years old."

Darby shrugged. "It's better than nothing. Giving us a distance is not strategic enough. If she can't do it, she'll let us know."

After a moment, Maisie replied at a low volume that sounded strange because it wasn't really a whisper. "Two unknown humans located inside four-story building. One human located at street level. Room coordinates from this location are northeast. One human located on level four. Room coordinates from this location southwest."

"Do you detect any movement?" Darby asked.

"No. Humans are stable," she said.

"That's good news," I whispered. "We go in through the door above us." I gestured to the stairs. "Then converge on the room located to the northeast. Then move to the fourth floor." I patted my vest pocket. "As per the plan, I have the Babble on me, with two darts ready to go. We take one of them alive, inject them, and figure out what their orders are." I nodded at Darby. "I designate you as Maisie's official correspondent. You get the most out of her with the least amount of effort. Please ask her to search that door up there for any threats and have her look for any live video feed that might be set up in the building."

Darby nodded, heading up the stairs, conferring with Maisie.

"I don't like it," Bender grumbled as he came to stand next to me. "It's too easy. Something's off."

"Agreed," Lockland said, joining us. "Not having any traps rigged anywhere is suspicious. There's a possibility they know of Claire's involvement with us and know we'd arrive here at some point. Maybe they're not expecting us to show up in the basement, as they don't know we know about the medi-pod, but they are expecting us."

"That's a fair assumption," I said. "I figured by now we'd be engaged in some sort of firefight. It's too quiet for my liking. But we're here, and we have to continue on. There's no way they know we have a status reader, but we have to move quickly. Once the others are back from Claire's fake meeting, the situation will reverse. We have to be ready."

Lockland met my gaze, nodding once. "Let's go."

From the top of the stairs, Darby was gesturing wildly, his face animated. We hurried up to him. In a barely audible voice, he said, "Maisie detects an electromagnetic field behind here." He pointed at the door in front of us. "I'm not familiar with how it works, but the way she describes it, if anyone walks through it, they'll be electrocuted. All of the molecules in their body will be zapped instantaneously."

"That's not good," I said. "Did she offer up a plan?"

He glanced around sheepishly. "I didn't ask." He brought the status reader up to his lips. "Please state an alternative way of entry, or a way to deactivate electromagnetic field. Answer at lowest decibel setting for human hearing."

Maisie's reply was so faint, Darby had to practically smash the egg to his ear. I cocked my head closer to listen, barely able to make out her words. "Electromagnetic field can be grounded by copper wire located below in cabinet near medi-pod. Peel back protective coating on each end. Insert one end under the door on the right. Insert the other to the left. Step back to avoid further contact. Current will exceed capacity. Coating will melt. Fire probable. Time allotted for entry is one minute, twelve seconds."

Without a word, I headed down the stairs in search of the wire. The cabinets were mounted along one wall. I started from the left and made my way right, finding the wire in the third storage bin. Unraveling three meters, I cut it with my blade, hurrying back up the steps as I peeled back the coating on one end.

Once I was done, I handed it to Darby. He looked aghast, glancing at the copper wire like it would bite him. "You want me…to do it? The voltage is crazy high. One mistake and my insides sizzle."

"Darb, you're our science engineer. We have to be ready with our weapons once we open that door."

"I'll do it," Lockland whispered, reaching for the wire.

"No." Darby shook his head. "Holly's right. I can." He stuffed Maisie in his pocket and got down on his knees. The crack under the door was only three centimeters. He angled his head to the floor so he could see better.

I nudged his shoulder, handing him my macro-glasses. "I know you can do this."

He donned the glasses and peered under the door again. "I think I see the rod that's producing the energy field. It's mounted just above the floor." He began threading one end of the copper wire underneath the door on the right. Once he was done with that side, he shuffled his body to the left, staying on his knees. "This is the tricky part," he whispered. "I only have one chance to secure it, then I let go, or I risk getting fried." His hands began to work, and almost immediately, there was a popping sound. Darby flung himself back like he'd been hit by a bullet. The wire began to hiss and smoke. Angry buzzing noises came from inside the door as Darby stumbled to his feet. "Do not step on that wire if you value your life."

We all took a step back.

"There's no way they don't hear that," Lockland said, flipping his infrared visor down. We all followed suit. "We move on three." Lockland raised his arm and swiped it down after three, grabbing on to the door handle.

Nothing happened. It was locked.

Bender moved forward, lifting his leg and smashing his boot into the housing next to the handle. The door popped open. No reinforced locks behind the force field. That was a shame for them.

We rushed into the room, knowing our entry had made enough noise to alert them of our presence, sweeping our weapons up, across, and down, checking for anything that could potentially harm us.

Lockland led the way in the direction Maisie had given us.

A call came from the hallway. "Grif, is that you?" It was a woman, which was mildly surprising.

Lockland motioned for us to fan out, taking cover behind the door, so she wouldn't see us unless she entered the room.

"The live feed just blinked out again," the woman said. "Albert said he was going to fix that short." She sounded mildly innocent and unarmed, but it could be a ploy.

If shorting out the electromagnetic field had triggered an outage in the building, we might've just saved ourselves from this woman ringing the alarm for the rest of the group.

With my back against the wall, I slid toward the opening, nodding at Lockland as I holstered my Gem.

"Grif? Are you in here?" the woman said, taking a step into the room.

I grabbed her by the arm, twisting her so her back was tight against my chest, my elbow locking around her neck, one hand covering her mouth. I didn't need to point my weapon at her, because the Blaster, Pulse, Web, and HydroSol held by everyone else were enough. "Don't say a word," I whispered in her ear. "If you value living and breathing for another five minutes, don't make a sound."

Movement sounded from upstairs.

Lockland stepped forward, the barrel of his Blaster aimed directly at her forehead. If he were to shoot, he'd kill both of us, but as long as she believed the threat, we were fine. Darby edged forward, exchanging the HydroSol for his taser. He knew that was the only thing that would leave me unscathed if the woman had to be shot.

"Is the man upstairs the only other person in this building?" Lockland asked. "If you lie, we will kill you."

She slowly nodded.

"Ask him to come down here," Lockland ordered.

I shook my head, indicating I didn't think we could trust her not to reveal our position.

Lockland placed the Blaster against her skull, pushing her head backward. "Ask him to come down here, and sound convincing. If you don't, I will insert this into your ear canal." He showed her a long, skinny tube that he'd taken from his pocket. "It won't kill you immediately, but you will wish you were dead. Nod if you understand."

She nodded. I wasn't going to interfere again.

As I unwrapped my hand from her mouth, she took in a breath. Lockland placed the tube inside her ear, exerting enough pressure to make her wince. What we were doing was critical for the well-being of thousands of people in the city. It was essential that we didn't let the situation get away from us.

I didn't often get to witness Lockland's interrogation techniques, but I was finding this one to be pretty effective.

For some, like Freedom, it never would've worked.

Her voice rang with unsteadiness. "Grif?" she called. I gripped her side, pressing hard to make her understand that she had to get it together, or she would receive a brainful of titanium. She stiffened, clearing her throat, and raised her voice a little. "Hey, Grif, can you come down here? We have another short in the system. The video feed is locked up." Much better.

Heavy footsteps trod down the stairs. "Haven? Is that you? I'm not supposed to leave my post. The guys should be back soon."

"I'm sorry to call you away," she said. "But there's another short in the system. Can you help?" As soon as her mouth closed, she began to sob silently, barely making a sound. This man meant something to her. But she wasn't going to ask us to save him. She knew what was at stake as well as we did.

As Grif came down the stairs, the pace of his steps increased. But as he neared the room where we waited, he hesitated.

We all heard it.

My hand was back around the woman's mouth, but she had stopped crying. Bender edged forward, repositioning himself down on one knee, aiming at the doorway with his Web laser, which shot hot light in a web pattern. It was an effective weapon to disable many at once, as the laser was broken up into small, individual units, but it wasn't as effective as a concentrated blast. For most anyway. Bender had perfected killing a single person with his trigger pattern and wrist movements.

Before Bender could shoot, laser fire hit the doorjamb, exploding around us.

As I maneuvered myself and Haven out of the way, she hooked her ankle around the back of my calf, bending quickly, trying to flip me over her shoulder. She'd taken me by surprise and would've been successful if she'd been a little heavier than I was.

Damn. I'd underestimated her when I knew what it was like to be constantly underestimated as a woman. I'd fallen for her soft voice and tears.

Stupid, stupid, stupid.

Bender and Lockland returned fire as I grappled with her. We tumbled to the ground, but before I could adjust my hold on her, she slid her hand into her pocket.

I heard the telltale click of a hydro-grenade a second later.

"She's rigged!" I yelled.

Case was over us in the next instant, hauling her up and tossing her into the hallway where Grif was firing on us.

We all dived to the other side of the room.

A hundred kilos collided into me as the explosion ripped through the room a second later.

Chapter 26

My ears rang as I blinked. The weight on top of me shifted and groaned. "Case?" I said, rolling him off me. "Are you hurt?" He'd covered me on the way down.

He sprawled on his back, his arms wide, breathing hard. "I don't think so. Other than having the wind knocked out of me."

I sat up, glancing around.

By the looks of it, Haven had made it partway back into the room before the hydro-grenade in her pocket exploded. Just about every surface was covered in red, sticky goo. I'd never seen anything like it.

Beside me, Lockland shuffled to his feet, shaking his head. Bender was farther away, groaning. The only one I couldn't see was Darby. From my vantage point, it looked like Grif hadn't fared too well from his position in the hallway.

Lockland moved toward the doorway. "We're going to need to amend our defense tactics," he said. "People who are eager and willing to die must be handled a different way."

"Agreed." I stood with the help of the wall, my ears aching and my head throbbing. "Darby? Where are you?" A loud moan came from behind a seating unit closer to the door. It was the only big piece of furniture in the room. I moved that way, my arms cartwheeling as I began to slip in the mess Haven had left behind. It was disgusting. Once at the couch, I didn't want to touch it. The thing was covered in red spray. "Just tell me if you're hurt. I can't see you."

"I'm okay," he muttered. "At least, I think I am."

Bender sat up, rubbing his head. I made my way toward him. "Is that your blood? Or hers?"

He brought his hand in front of his face to examine it, squinting. "Mine. I think. Well, mine mixed with her fucking body parts. I gashed my head on that table when the explosion tossed me." He gestured at the piece of furniture that was now in fragments on the floor next to him. "I can't believe these assholes want to die that bad. I don't get it."

"I don't either. Ending yourself without even knowing if you took out your adversary makes no sense. We all survived, and those two are dead." Everyone I'd ever known spent their entire life trying to survive in this rotten, drizzly, iron-caked world. It was all we did all day, every day. To end it without thought or a fight didn't correlate in my mind. "Whoever indoctrinated these people led them astray." I walked over and put a hand out to Case. He grasped it, and I hauled him up, both of us stumbling a little. "Thanks for covering me," I said. "That hydro-grenade was macro. We're extremely lucky." Grenades were ultracondensed, so their explosion diameter was greater than a regular bomb of the same size.

Case shrugged as he began to swipe blood and bits off his coat in long strokes with his gloves, flinging the gore to the ground. "I figured there was no reason for both of us to go."

It made sense to me. "Well, I appreciate it."

Darby made his way out from behind the seating unit. I moved toward him, grabbing his arm to stabilize him. The status egg had been in his pocket. "Maisie," I called, "tell me you're okay. If you're not, Daze might not forgive me."

She replied, "I am in stable condition. My polymer coating is military grade. Hydro-grenade explosion detected. Severe damage and loss of life within two-point-five meters of detonation."

"That is correct," I said. "Are there any other humans in this building besides us?"

"There are no other humans in this building. Only human remains."

I was relieved I didn't have to tell Daze that his favorite thing of all time had been destroyed.

Lockland made it to Grif in the hall. The man whose face we'd never seen was nothing more than a blown-out carcass.

"Come on." Lockland brought his arm up. "Let's find where their operations are and see if we can locate the others in the group before they arrive back. There's no way we're hiding this mess, so we need to be ready when they return."

We all stumbled after him, slipping and sliding as we went. I helped Darby, steering him through the doorway. He made a retching noise, covering his mouth, as we passed Grif. "What a horrible way to go."

I said, "At least it was quick."

"Quick and *disgusting*."

"I'm just glad that wasn't one of us," I told him.

From his position down the hallway, Lockland called, "I found a room with monitors."

We all converged in the small space, which had several displays set up. This was where Haven had to have been sitting before she'd heard us come through the electromagnetic-rigged door.

Bender pointed at one of the screens. "That's the medi-pod room, for fuck's sake. She knew we were here!"

I bent over to examine the image. Sure enough, it showed the medi-pod and the hole we'd made with the laser. We'd asked Maisie to detect live feed, and she'd failed to find their cameras. Either Darby hadn't been specific enough, or the video cameras had been altered enough to fool her database. "Why didn't she alert Grif we were in the building? She had enough time. It took us a while to short-circuit the electromagnetic field."

"My guess is she was trying to protect him," Case said. "She seemed the wrong temperament to be put in charge."

I pulled out a chair in front of the monitor and sat. "I don't think she was in charge. She was probably left here to ring the alarm. But when she saw us come in, she must've panicked about how to handle it. The bureau has probably never been infiltrated before, and clearly they weren't expecting us this morning, or they would've left someone more competent."

"Grif might've been her lover," Darby added. "She seemed so sad in the end when she knew that he would probably die. I felt bad for her."

"I did, too," I said. "Which almost cost us our lives. I underestimated her, and by doing so, I allowed her to get her hand in her pocket. It was my fault we were almost blown up. I'm sorry. It won't happen again." I noticed movement on one of the screens. This particular camera appeared to be focused on the short hallway between the two buildings. "It looks like someone is coming through the tunnel from the housing building."

Everyone leaned forward.

Bender growled, "If they go through that door—"

The hydro-bomb Bender had fastened to the handle exploded.

Then the monitor went black.

"The explosion took out the camera, which means it was located close to the door," Lockland said. "We have to assume there will be more people coming behind that person. Darby, you stay here and try to figure out where their communication devices are. We know they have a private bandwidth, and we need to find out how they're communicating, so we can listen in. The rest of us will scout the building. Yell if you see anything on the monitors." Once the four of us were out in the hallway, Lockland continued, "There are two staircases. Bender and I will take this one, you two take the other." He nodded down the corridor. "You know what to look for. We need intel on anything they have, such as other monitoring equipment, weapons, antennas, and the like. Anything that will help us ascertain their current location."

"Got it. We'll meet back down here in ten," I said. "I want to be front and center when the others arrive home."

Bender nodded. "Good luck."

Case and I started down the hallway, skirting what was left of Grif. "Of course they make us go this way, while they got the clean stairway," I said.

We both had our weapons drawn. This was the first time I noticed the building was in good shape—really good shape. In fact, it was one of the most put-together buildings I'd ever seen. "This place looks almost how I would imagine it looked before the dark days. Not only has it been cleaned of debris, but they've cobbled it back together with decent materials."

We started up the stairs. "Yeah, I noticed," Case murmured, sweeping his arms back and forth, prepared to encounter a threat Maisie hadn't foreseen. "They definitely had access to resources nobody else had over the years. The materials don't match the original, but they did a damn good job with what they had."

We reached the second-floor landing.

I angled my body one way as Case's attention went the other. There were only three doors in this section and a wall separating the rest of the floor. Bender and Lockland were investigating the other side.

The first door was open, no detectable movement inside. A cursory glance showed it was a bedroom with no other doors and a single sleeping pod. The next door was partially ajar. A waste room. Case went in and gave the all clear. The next door was shut.

"My guess is it's another sleeping room," I whispered. "You open it, I'll cover." Case stretched to reach the handle, clicking it down, pushing it open with his boot.

Just as I suspected, it contained two sleeping pods. There were personal items littered about—a shirt, a trinket, some random hygiene products. We moved into the room. "This is a living level," Case said. "We're not going to find much here. Let's head to the next floor."

On the third level, we found more of the same. Two sleeping rooms and a waste room. On the fourth level, we found what we were looking for. The first room was likely where Grif had been before he'd come down. It was full of monitors, but these didn't have live video feeds. They were older computer screens hooked to static hubs. They were not as fast or as efficient as a pico, but they had access to large databases and could do calculations.

I sat down in one of the chairs. Numbers and

formulas were on the screen. "This is where they communicate with the S17 militia," Case said. I turned to look. He stood in front of a large amplifier. "Look, the antenna goes up the side of the wall and into the roof. That's how they get the distance."

A shout came from downstairs.

Case and I took off, making it down the stairs within seconds. It was Darby. We headed toward the room where we'd left him, almost colliding with Bender and Lockland, who had rushed back down the other staircase.

"What is it?" I asked as we all clambered into the room.

Darby turned in his seat, looking pale. "I think…I think…"

"This is so not the time to go nonverbal. What is it?" I refrained from putting my hands on his shoulders to shake him.

"I think they're gone."

"Who's gone?" I asked.

"I don't think anyone was waiting for us to arrive in The North," he said. "Look, I found Haven's status reports." He motioned to the monitor behind him. Instead of a live video feed, there were words on the screen. "She tried to encrypt them, but it was easy to hack. The twelve members left quickly, tasking a few people to stay behind, like Haven, Grif, and somebody named Port, who may have just died downstairs. Port was their backup, in charge of setting off bombs if need be. But it wasn't clear if he had them on his body, or if they were already here. It appears Haven may have signaled him. But they suspected Claire all along. Once she called a meeting and told them we were going to be in The North, they figured the info was false. For some unknown reason, they decided to vacate the premises right after. According to Haven's notes, they weren't entirely sure we'd come here, but knew our entre back into the city would bring trouble, which is why I believe she was indecisive about what to do."

"Do you think Claire is safe?" I asked.

"Yes," Darby said. "They didn't want to arouse any suspicion, and according to this, they left quickly and quietly."

"So where did the bastards go?" Bender asked.

Darby shrugged. "Her notes didn't include that. But I'm assuming they went to rendezvous with Tillman and the militia. I can keep checking. There's bound to be more information here somewhere, possibly journal entries by others."

Lockland sat in a seat across from Darby, his visor up, his face drawn. "I believe this outcome was unavoidable," he said in a resolute tone. "Even if we had been able to take most of them out today, word would've likely gotten through to Tillman, or someone would've slipped by our arsenal. We tried our best to contain the situation, but this is what it is. We have to face facts and realize that the odds aren't in our favor any longer. This is going to be a long fight."

I leaned back against a wall, tugging off my helmet. Exhaustion and emotion flowed through me. "Well, there is a bright side. By vacating the city, they are giving us time to plan a counterattack. They've basically relinquished this building, including the medi-pod." I wiped the back of my hand along my brow. "They don't know about the scientists, or their resources, and they don't know we know what that medi-pod can do."

"Yes." Case nodded. "They understood that showing their hand and exposing themselves before they were ready meant that they would lose. It gave us an advantage."

Bender said, "We also have that asshole Reed, and Claire and the rest of the loyalists will be able to give us the names of those missing, so we will know exactly who they are."

"Yes," Darby said. "The first thing we need to do is bring Mary here and assess whether the medi-pod works. If it does, we can cure more seekers, and if we can do that, we can gather more and more people on our side, building up a strong alliance."

"That will give us time to develop an adequate plan to defeat this militia before they arrive here," Lockland said.

I glanced down at my boots, which were covered in red grime. "I don't think they'll come back here," I said. "They know we have hidey-holes and weapon stashes all over the city. They might not know exactly where, but they know we have access to an arsenal. They also know that we will be able to convince people to follow us. They won't risk it. If we were in their position, we wouldn't either."

"They have no leverage to lure us out of the city," Lockland said. "Which is the only other option."

Pushing off from the wall, I shrugged. "Give them time and they'll do something to make us come for them. They need us gone before they can resume their plans. If we achieve our goals of gathering support, they lose." I bent over one of the monitors again. "We have to remain vigilant. We can't give them any opportunity to get us out of town before we're ready. That means we keep a low profile and remain on high alert continuously. None of us can go back to our residences, or any of our known haunts." Bender grunted. "That means you, too." I bobbed my head in his direction. "Your place is the most visible, and don't forget, we're referred to as *Bender's crew*. That's how they see us. If they were going to try to pick one of us up, they'd stake out your place first."

"So, what's the short-term plan moving forward?" Darby asked.

"In my opinion"—I glanced around the group—"we gather Claire and a few people she trusts and install them in here immediately. Then we pick up Daze and Reed. We're bound to get more useful information from Reed." I met Lockland's eyes. "Mary needs to be in the medi-pod as soon as possible, just like Darby said. After that, we gather as much intel as we possibly can. Then we ready a solid plan and take a trip down South to meet with the scientists. After that, we strike."

Lockland nodded. "We scour this building from top to bottom, nothing left unturned. We make sure this place is not rigged with even the smallest hazard, then we go get everyone. If this is going to become our new base of operations, Bender and I need to hit a few of our remote places to gather some supplies."

Case added, "I'll retrieve Daze and Reed and enough dried food to last us a few weeks."

"After we're done with the sweep, I'll head to Ned and Mary," I said.

"I'll track down Claire and explain everything," Darby said. "She said she would either be at her office or her residence. I can get there by walking. I'll go through the other building, so I don't attract attention."

"Sounds good," I agreed. "We move with caution, but we move quickly. We're not sure if they even know we've taken this building yet, since Haven didn't sound the alarms. But they'll know soon enough." Everyone nodded. "After the hazard check, we take one hour. No more."

Chapter 27

I held Mary in my arms. We'd sedated her with Quell before moving her. She hadn't been doing well in the little room she and Ned had been forced to hide out in, so I was relieved to have her here. I laid her gently in the medi-pod.

Darby, Claire, and Ned stood next to me.

I'd made it back before Lockland, Bender, and Case.

Even though I'd entered the canals on foot, I'd risked getting Luce out of the basement of Yazzie, where she'd been stored for a while, to transport Mary. I'd parked my craft a few blocks away from the Emporium. Ned and I had carried Mary down the street and loaded her into Luce, which was now parked in a deserted building half a kilometer from here. I'd had no choice. I'd move her later.

Lockland and Bender had gone on their errands on foot, and Case had headed to the east entrance to get Seven to fly to the barracks. We'd been lucky enough to take off shortly after we adjourned the meeting, having cleared the building with Maisie's help in under fifteen minutes. We hadn't found much, other than a cache of guns and bombs. Nothing had been rigged to blow, which had proved we'd taken them by surprise. They hadn't expected us to come to them. I loved it when that happened.

"Have you had time to examine the machine?" I asked Darby as he closed the lid.

"A bit," he said. "It looks to be in good working condition. We were lucky that Bender aimed that hydro-bomb out into the hallway, rather than into this room. There was minimal damage." I glanced over at the blown-out wall. There hadn't been much of a body left.

"Don't worry, nobody's coming in that way," Claire said. "We've secured the housing building next door and this one under the quarantine laws." She grinned. "Those who've gone missing are now thought to be under quarantine for a deadly plague making its way around the city. That should keep down the gossip for a while and give us a few days to figure out all the bureau players." Plagues were fairly common, and so was mandatory quarantine. It hadn't happened in a few years, but people understood what to expect and generally stayed in their homes. The housing building was now full of loyalists, who were sorting out the identities of the individuals with the bureau, so we'd have names and faces.

I glanced at Mary, who appeared peaceful for the

first time in a while. "Is there a *Cure Seeker* button?" I asked, hoping this was going to be easy.

"No," Darby said. "But there is a *Diagnose* button. We'll start with that." He hit the dial, and the thing roared to life, much like the one we'd used to heal Bender and Lockland.

I raised an eyebrow. "Does this thing run on liquid hydrogen, too?" I made a move to look behind it.

He shook his head. "No, something even bigger."

"What's bigger than liquid fuel?"

"A fusion reactor."

My eyes widened. "Are you sure?" Fusion had been a revolutionary invention for our ancestors. A super-efficient energy source, it had required a tremendous amount of energy to start, but once the chain reaction began, it generated an unbelievable amount of energy. The fusion technology hadn't survived the aftermath of the meteor, because even though it had worked well, it was fragile. I'd never uncovered a working fusion reactor in all my years of salvaging.

"Yes, I'm sure," Darby said. "In order to operate all the precision lasers and magnetic responders, and do the kind of work that needs to be done inside a body at that level, nothing less than a fusion reaction would work. I was skeptical that this would have it, but it does. All the other machines had their energy source stripped by the time we got to them, so I had no idea what they used." He walked to the other side while the pod continued to whir and opened a metal screen on the bottom. "It doesn't look that old either. They must've had some incredibly talented people on the team designing these and putting them together, taking remnants that survived and converting them into a working unit."

I glanced inside the reactor, which contained a smooth cylindrical glass enclosure clouded by the energy it was making. Darby shut the screen. "They achieved something amazing, and it cost them their lives," I said.

"Now that she's in there," Claire said as we came around the front, "I'm going to head to the housing building next door. Let me know when Lockland and Bender arrive. There's a lot of work to be done. The loyalists are upbeat. They're happy with how this turned out. Nobody was ready for battle."

I nodded. "We're going to need your smartest and brightest involved. Darby already got through one encryption, but they had to have left behind more information. And once Case brings Reed back, we can interrogate him together."

"I look forward to that," Claire said. "We need to figure out who these assholes are and stop them, once and for all."

When Claire swore, you knew things were about to go down. "Agreed. Getting more information is vitally important."

"I'll continue to work on it from my end," she said. "People gossip. People talk. Haven was a regular government worker who'd been with us for at least ten years. They'd recruited her recently."

"As well as Grif?" I asked.

She shook her head. "No, if I had to guess, Grif Manalow had ties to the organization for a long time. He wasn't a loyalist, but there'd been enough talk about him over the years to know he didn't support the government as it stood. The two of them hooked up less than a year ago. They were lovers."

"I figured as much," I said. "The entire thing is sad. Why they would forfeit their lives like that makes no sense."

Claire gave me a brief hug and nodded at Ned and Darby, heading toward the exposed hole in the wall. "People like that defy intelligence."

I took out my timepiece for the second time since I'd been back, trying not to worry. It was going on an hour. In front of us, the medi-pod began to slow. "Already?" I stuck the clock back in my pocket. "That was quick."

Ned, who'd been standing off to the side, came forward. "What does it say? Is she going to be okay?" Each word was stressed.

Darby examined the digital display. "It went fast, because this medi-pod was especially designed for seekers. All it had to do was confirm her DNA had been altered in a way consistent with Plush damage to know what's wrong with her." He pointed at the screen. "See? It says, 'seeker profile identified.'"

"Okay, what now?" I asked.

"Yeah," Ned chimed in. "What happens next?"

"It says to hit the *Cure* button," he said. "How quickly her DNA can be restored will depend on her health profile, integrity of her organs, resiliency, and a few other factors."

"Can you give us a time frame?" I asked.

"Not really. It states here"—Darby's head was bent over the screen—"that it could take anywhere from one day to a full week. After that, it says…" His voice trailed off.

"What?" I knew that tone. "What's wrong?" I asked.

He brought his head up. "After a week, it says the seeker can no longer be saved. That either their body will not survive the treatment, or the damage is too severe for even this medi-pod to fix."

Damn. That wasn't what we wanted to hear. So, for the most part, seekers who'd been infected for years would have a lesser chance of surviving.

I settled a hand on his arm. "Darb, we have to focus on the positive," I told him. "The fact that this pod is here, in working condition, and can help people is completely amazing. A significant amount of souls will be cured, I know it."

"But…but…" Darby stammered. "Those who can't be healed. We'll have to—"

"Darby." I steered him away from the machine, placing my hands on his shoulders. "We don't have to make any decisions right now. Let's focus on Mary. One thing at a time. I promise you it's going to be okay. There will be happiness, and there will be sorrow. That sums up our lives in this era. We're lucky enough to be a part of reshaping this world and helping people. We have to concentrate on that."

"I know," he said. "It's just hard." He snuck a glance over his shoulder. "This medi-pod was expertly designed and has so much power. I wanted it to work for everyone."

"I did, too," I agreed.

A noise sounded from above as the former electromagnetic-protected door opened. Reflexively, I drew my Gem, aiming it upward.

Lockland came through first, followed by Bender.

"Somebody's going to have to clean that shit up in there." Bender gestured with a thumb over his shoulder. "We can't live in a place with body parts sprayed all over the walls."

"Claire's on it," I said, holstering my weapon. "She's going to bring some people in with Bang. It should be cleaned up by tonight." Bang was our universal cleaner. It disintegrated any organic substance it came in contact with. Getting it on your skin was a no-no.

Lockland gestured toward the medi-pod as he came down the stairs. "I'm assuming she's inside?"

"She is," I said. "Darby was just about to hit *Cure*." I nudged Darby back toward the pod, and he reached out, depressing the button. The thing began to whirl. "She was diagnosed with a seeker profile already, and we're going from there. It could take a day or a week, depending on her health and the amount of damage." I'd fill them in on the rest of it later. "Are the supplies upstairs?"

"Yes," Lockland said. "We got everything we needed. Case back yet?"

"No," I said. "I'm giving him five more minutes. If they don't come through that door by then, I'm going after them. Luce is parked about six blocks from here. We set an hour, because it was a realistic time frame for us to achieve our goals. If they were tied up, Case would've used the tech phone. Nothing's come through."

Lockland pulled off his helmet, running a hand through his short hair. "You're right. You should check on them."

"I'm assuming they're not in any serious trouble, but Case might be having issues with Reed. Maybe the guy woke up and hassled Daze. I don't know, but something's going on. Whatever it is, the kid might be freaked out." I took my timepiece out again. It'd been three minutes, not five, but I made up my mind. "I'm going after them." I turned to Darby. "I'm rooting for Mary. I'm sure she'll come out of this just fine. She hasn't been infected that long."

"I'm sure she will, too," he replied. "Be careful." He took my HydroSol out of his waistband and handed it to me. "You might need this."

I nodded, taking it and heading for the stairs, passing Bender.

"If you're not back in an hour," he said, "we'll come to you."

"I know."

Luce was in the air five minutes later.

"Daze! Case!" I yelled as I ran through the blown-out entry to the barracks. I'd parked Luce in Seven's spot, figuring they must've already taken off before I arrived, when I noticed the entire front door was missing. The door that had been a solid meter thick and made of some of the heaviest steel I'd ever seen.

Trying not to be completely panicked, my heart racing, I entered the main barracks area with my Gem in one hand and the HydroSol in the other.

It was pitch black inside.

My visor was down, and with the light streaming in from the blown door, I was able to see enough.

The place was trashed.

Crates had been upended. The cooling unit was on its side, contents tumbling out. "Daze," I called, my voice filled with anxiety. "Are you here?"

Please, please, be here.

"Holly?" The door to the battery room creaked opened. Daze's voice broke when he saw me. "Holly!"

"Yes, it's me." I holstered my weapons as he came speeding toward me, flying into my arms. He buried his face in my neck, sobbing, his thin body quaking. I gave him a minute to recover before I peeled him back, stationing him in front of me as I knelt. "Daze, I know this is hard, but you have to tell me everything that happened, and I need you to do it fast."

"They came… They took them…" he managed between choking sounds.

Calmly, I asked, "Who came? Who took whom?"

"I didn't see them. I only saw their crafts when they

left!" he cried. "I'm so sorry! I couldn't help. Case stuffed me in the battery room. He made me lock the door. He told me to crawl onto the roof and stay there until I heard another craft. He knew you'd come back. He made me go! If he hadn't had to help me, he could've fought them off. But by the time he put me in there, they were here." He dove for me again, clutching me around the neck, quiet sobs racking his body.

I held him tightly, one hand cradling his head. "It's okay. *Shh.* It's going to be okay. When you're ready, you need to tell me everything." Case had possibly forfeited his life for Daze's, and for that I would be eternally grateful. But the outskirt couldn't be gone. I wasn't ready to accept that.

"Are they going to kill him?" Daze's mouth was muffled, tangled in my hair.

I gently tugged the kid back, unhooking his hands from behind my neck. "No, they're not. We're going to get him back," I said with surety.

We were fucking getting him back.

"He's the only bargaining chip they have," I said. "So they'll keep him alive." At least for a while. "They needed something to lure us down there, and they found that with Case, but them knowing about this place never entered my mind."

"I heard some stuff." Daze sniffled, running his forearm under his leaky nose. "Case wanted me to go right through the hatch, but I couldn't. I tried to listen. I wanted to help. They said Reed had a tracker in him and he was too stupid to know better. One guy said they lost his location close by, because the barracks is underground, but then Case flew back and they saw his craft. He came back for me! If he had just stayed away, he would've been safe!"

I shook my head. "No," I assured him. "If they tracked Reed to this area, they would've stuck around until they figured it out. This isn't your fault." If Tillman knew who Case was, because of his connection to Dixon, this was going to be bad for him. But I wasn't going to share that with the kid. "He's alive." I patted Daze's shoulder. "They will keep him alive." How long, however, was debatable.

"Are you sure you can bring him back?" His eyes were rimmed with red as tears continued streaming down his face.

"Yes," I answered fervently, even though that emotion didn't match how I was feeling on the inside. I smiled. "You want to know how I'm going to do it?"

"How?" His nose had begun to drip again.

"With Maisie," I said. "She knows Case. She can pick him out of a crowd of unknowns and give me his precise location, so I can get to him without being detected." And annihilate anyone standing in my way.

"Okay," he said, mopping his sleeve under his nose. "When are you going to leave? Soon?"

I stood, flipping my visor up. "Yes. I'm leaving right after I drop you off with the others." Time was critical. Each moment that passed, Case's life would be in further jeopardy. Plus, they wouldn't be expecting any kind of retaliation within a single day.

"You're going to make the guys who took him pay for what they did, right?"

I grabbed his hand, leading him out of the barracks toward Luce. "Oh, yes. And I'm going to make it hurt."

Chapter 1

"Going alone is too risky," Bender argued. "You heard Reed when we gave him Babble. He said his militia was one hundred and seventy-six strong, and Tillman, an imminent threat in his own right, has another thirty at least." Bender leaned against the wall, the whir of the medi-pod in the basement of the government building we stood in churned at a steady rate. Mary had been in there for at least two hours.

I stood in the middle of the room, arms crossed, facing off with my crew about the dangerous journey I was about to embark on whether they liked it or not. "I'm not backing down on this. If we don't take them by surprise, we lose any chance of saving Case." That wasn't going to happen. Daze stood near me, sniffling, still blaming himself for Case's capture. It seemed Reed, our unwilling Bureau of Truth former prisoner and informant, had been implanted with a tracking device. The militia had lost his signal when he'd entered the barracks, but had lain in wait until Case had arrived. By the time I'd gotten there they were already gone.

"This is my fault," Daze sniffed. "I'll go with Holly."

I settled a hand on his shoulder. "No one's going with me except Maisie. She's all I need, and if I don't leave now, Case could be dead by the time I get there." My gaze landed firmly on Lockland, then Darby, settling on Bender. Ned sat in a chair by the medi-pod, but he wasn't part of this discussion. "They have just over an hour head start as it stands right now. If I move soon, I can be right behind them. Maisie can help with the rest. She'll be able to locate Case's signature, differentiating it from the rest. This is not a war. This is me sneaking in, grabbing Case before they kill him, and getting out."

"It's not going to be that easy and you know it," Lockland said. "They're going to have that place on lockdown and they have access to tech we know nothing about. From what you told me from your view from the sky, it's a large concrete building that very well might be impenetrable."

"I never said this would be simple. And nothing is impenetrable, especially with the right gear," I said. "I'm the best chance Case has and we all know it." Lockland's face was set. "How about this, if Maisie can't find a way in with a greater than fifty percent success rate, I'll head back and we come up with a new plan. You have my word." When we'd broken into this building, we'd found that Maisie had the capacity to calculate odds when it came to mission operations. She was military after all.

"Fifty percent?" Darby balked from his position next to the medi-pod. "I was thinking more like eighty-seven. Why would you risk your life on fifty percent chance of survival?"

"I said greater than fifty," I replied. "I have to account for the fact Maisie will underestimate my skill level. She's a computer, after all. She's going to give me her recommendation based on combat success rates of average soldiers in her sixty plus year old database. That's not me." I took a step forward, dropping my arm off Daze's shoulder. "I'm going. We can argue about this, but it won't change my mind. Case would do the same for me. Hell, if I'd been taken someone would already be gone. I can tell you now that the percentage of success will go down considerably if anyone joins me. This is a one-woman operation, and after I get Case," my voice firm, "we're heading down to rendezvous with the scientists. Once the militia and Tillman find out he's gone, they will retaliate. We'll ready ourselves down there, and you ready yourselves up here. If they don't strike within a few days, we meet up."

Bender took a step forward. "I don't like it. I say one of us goes with you. You're going to need backup."

I shook my head. "The only thing working in our favor is stealth. More than one person and we lose that. Don't forget they have access to live video feed. I'm planning on sneaking in on the sly, not announcing myself. Maisie will be able to detect tech and individuals. I can do this, but I do it alone."

Lockland gave me a long look. Then he brought his

head down once. "Fine. I can see there's no changing your mind. But the percentage of success, according to Maisie, has to be greater than sixty percent."

"Fifty-five," I said.

He slowly shook his head. "Sixty."

"Fine," I grumbled. "I'll just bring enough firepower with me that Maisie ups the odds—"

The medi-pod began to slow, a green light flickering from the readout. I headed over, anxious to see if Mary was all right. Lockland and Bender followed as Daze squeezed in front. Green was good. At least I hoped it was.

"What does it say?" Daze asked, his voice conveying all our concern and anxiety. "Is she going to be okay?"

"Let's give Darby some space," I said, taking a small step back.

"The preliminary diagnostics look encouraging," Darby said. "It says eighty percent of the nucleotides have been repaired and are now functioning. Her liver and brain activity are almost normal."

A sound came from inside.

"Darb, open the top," I prodded.

Darby, flustered, fumbled with the latch and lofted the lid. This one wasn't all glass, like some of the others, so we couldn't see Mary's face.

I leaned over, Daze next to me, Ned peering down from the other side…

DANGER'S HUNT is available now! Don't miss out on the further adventures of Holly & her crew.

NOTHING IS CREATED WITHOUT A GREAT TEAM.

My thanks to:

Awesome Cover design: Damonza.com

Digital and print formatting: Author E.M.S

Copyedits/proofs: Joyce Lamb

Final proof: Marlene Engel

ABOUT THE AUTHOR

Amanda Carlson is a graduate of the University of Minnesota, with a BA in both Speech and Hearing Science & Child Development. She went on to get an A.A.S in Sign Language Interpreting and worked as an interpreter until her first child was born. She's the author of the high octane Jessica McClain urban fantasy series published by Orbit, the Sin City Collectors paranormal romance series, the contemporary fantasy Phoebe Meadows series, and the futuristic/dystopian Holly Danger series. Look for these books in stores everywhere. She lives in Minneapolis with her husband and three kids.

Find her all over social media

Website: amandacarlson.com
Facebook: facebook.com/authoramandacarlson
Twitter: @amandaccarlson
Instagram: @author_amanda